private eyes

rene fomby

Book Ness
Monster
Press

Book Ness Monster Press
4530 Blue Ridge Drive
Belton, Texas 76513

Paperback ISBN: 9781947304031

Visit us on the World Wide Web: http://www.renefomby.com

Fomby, Rene. Private Eyes. Book Ness Monster Press.
Paperback Edition.

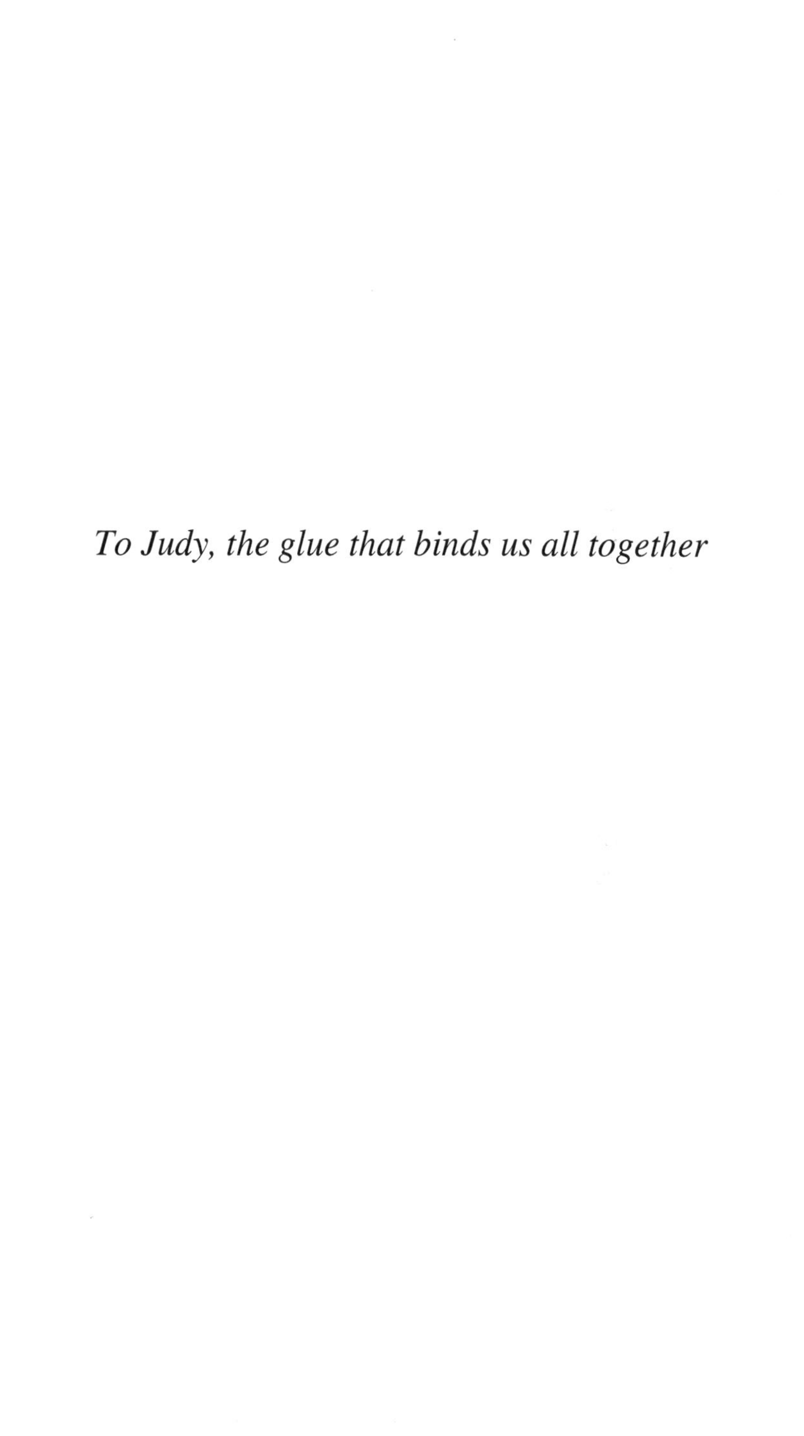

To Judy, the glue that binds us all together

Downtown Chicago, Early Saturday Morning

He's just sitting there, slouched on top of his desk, checking me out. He's grossly obese, fat hanging in rolls off his stomach, the hair on his ears spiked up like he's growing horns. A fat and stubby cigar squats in an ashtray beside him, unlit. The morning sun is finally showing its face over the tops of the buildings across the street, flooding in from a window just behind him, making it almost impossible to see his face. Probably all intentional on his part. His name is Antonio, but the street just calls him Fat Tony. Not that I'd risk calling him that to his face.

I'm not quite sure what I'm supposed to do at this point, so I pick out a chair parked right in front of him and hop on in. A good idea because it puts me more on his level, eye to eye. Finally, after what seems like almost an eternity to me, he leans forward and breaks the silence.

"Listen up. I'm a doer, not a talker, so I'm only gonna say this once." He stops to clear his throat, and coughs up something brown and disgusting into the ashtray, just missing the cigar. "First off, let me say I'm surprised to see you here. We don't get many of your kind around these parts. It's not natural, if you catch my drift."

He sounds like a poor imitation of Owen Wilson playing Marlon Brando playing the Godfather. His accent fades in and out as he speaks, so it's clear to me that it's all just an act. But I need this guy — desperately — so I play along. "Yeah, well, I thought about going with the other guys, but you come highly recommended, and this case is just too important to risk someone else screwing it up." As a matter of fact, I would have felt a lot more comfortable working with "the other guys," and hiring Antonio isn't going to do much for my reputation back home, but if I can somehow save Killer's hide, it'll be worth it. Killer will make sure no one gives me any grief over it. Nobody messes with Killer. Nobody.

He smiles at me, but I'm not really feeling any warmth. "Well, well, despite the looks o' ya, maybe you got some smarts after all. And just so's you know, we're not all that prejudiced around here. I mean, I've met one or two of your people who turned out to be pretty up-and-up guys, and I've even been known to hire a few of your type every now and then. Purely for muscle, ya know, not for anything that takes any real brains."

I'm not really feeling the love at this point, sitting here being insulted by the likes of him. I have half a mind to just get up and bug out, take my business across town. But then I think of Killer, sitting there on death row, probably doing solitary while he waits for the needle that could come for him any day now. Unless I can prove that he didn't do it, that he was framed. I gotta see this thing through, regardless of what I have to take off this fat cat. I gotta do it for Killer.

"So, watcha got? Somebody stole your girl?" Antonio has an annoying smirk on his face. Or maybe that's just how he looks all the time. It's hard to tell with his kind of people. That whole inscrutable thing. I decide to just ignore it for now. “No, this is really big. Pal of mine got into some serious trouble, wound up accused of offing a Frenchie he was seeing. Cute little thing, but I always told him she was trouble with a capital T. Those Frenchies always are. Anyway, she wound up dead, and they found her all torn up, bleeding out onto the sidewalk. Got her to the hospital, but it was too late. Then they went looking for the guy who did it, and my buddy was the first place they looked. I suppose it’s partly because of the reputation — his people always get fingered when there’s violence involved. It’s all just profiling, you know, but that doesn’t mean a thing when the man comes for you, when he’s got you in his net. Somebody gets hurt, somebody has to pay. That’s just the way it is these days.”

“Hey, people want justice,” Fat Tony suggests, spreading his arms in a wide, encompassing gesture.

“No, it’s not about justice. It should be about getting the right guy, about making sure you got the real killer off the streets. But at the end of the day, it's nothing more than an excuse for locking them all up. And it's working. The jails are chock full of his kind, thrown in the pen like wild animals with no chance of ever seeing daylight again."

He looks a little more interested now. "So they have your buddy in custody, eh? Where at?"

"Southside," I tell him, hanging my head.

He lets out a low whistle. "Southside? That's one rough place. He in the general population?"

I shake my head. "Nah, I don't think so, not given what's he's accused of. I'd imagine they've got him in his own cage, in solitary, where he can't hurt nobody else. They're going through all the paperwork now, but I don't think he's got much time left before everything's in order and they come for him. You know..."

"Yeah, I know. The needle." He taps the desktop in front of him, thinking. "So, what's this guy's name? And how well do you know him?"

"His name is Killer." He gives me a startled look. "Yeah, I know, but he didn't name himself, if you know what I mean. Some people just don't seem to think when they pick names, don't realize what kind of trouble that can lead to down the road. But he's not like that at all. He's really just a pussycat inside." I see the narrowed eyes and realize my mistake right away. "No, no, no offense. I just mean he's a really gentle soul. Wouldn't hurt a fly, really. Nothing like what most people think of when they hear his breed…"

"Pit bull."

"Yeah, right, pit bull. But I think he's got a touch of Lab in him, too. Maybe that's what makes him so sweet. Labs are just born that way, I guess. Anyway, I've known the guy all my life, ever since I lost my Mom. Lives just a few doors down from me. I've got a secret spot out back that I can scoot through to make my rounds. Matter of fact, that's how I got free to come see you this morning. It's hidden behind a bush where the humans can't see it. Anyway, Killer and I would hang out together most days, just shooting the bull, as it were. Shooting the bull, get it? Pit bull, shooting the—"

"Yeah, yeah, I get it."

Antonio looks annoyed, and starts licking a paw and wiping his head. I remember too late that his people aren't exactly known for their sense of humor. Kind of grumpy, in fact. If we're being honest. "Yeah, well, anyway, that's pretty much the way it's been the last six years or so, just me and Killer, best pals. Then this Frenchie moves into the neighborhood, and everything changed. She's got that certain *smell* to her, if you know what I mean. Drives guys wild. Or at least the guys who still, you know…"

"Still have something left to howl about. I get it. I take it you don't?"

"No, no, that all got taken care of when I was adopted." I can't help but glance down for a second, remembering the operation. With no painkillers, no anesthesia. Treated like some kind of animal. "Had no say in the matter, to be honest. Although, seeing as how that all played out for Killer, I can't say I'm all that unhappy about the situation."

Antonio gives me a funny, pathetic look. "Spoken like a man who's never known the difference. I tell ya, son, I'd have clawed their eyes out if they came for mine." He pauses, looking wistfully off in the distance. "Yeah, I'm a little old for all that nonsense now, but back in the day I was known as a real ladies man, a regular tomcat. I remember this certain Persian girl, fur soft as silk, with a tail on her some guys would kill for…"

I clear my throat, getting his attention. "Well, sir, that's why I'm here. Somebody killed my pal's girl and framed him for it, and now we've only got a day or so before he goes down for the last ride. So time is wasting here. We've got to hit the streets like yesterday and find the real killer before Killer gets put down. And to make things worse, I'm pretty sure I've only got a couple hours before my mug is plastered up on every telephone pole from Joliet to Evanston."

Antonio shakes his head, fully alert now. It looks like I've finally gotten through to him. "Okay. About that." He waves a plump paw in my direction.

"I need a little more information, and then I'm ready to go to work. In the meantime, you can just go home and hang out until I got something for ya."

I sit up stiffly and look him straight in the eye, showing him I mean business. "That isn't going to work for me, Antonio. First of all, we need to move fast on this, so we need as many paws on the ground as we can get. But even more importantly, you're going to be moving around in certain neighborhoods and talking to certain people who aren't, how shall we say it, exactly *friendly* to your kind. So you're going to need someone who's got your back, someone who can vouch for you with the locals. Someone those folks know and can trust. And that would be me."

"Look, I hear ya, *mi amico*. But the thing is, there's a reason you came to see me, and not Sal Monella and his crew. Caninvestigators. No offense, but the problem with dogs is, they're great for nosing around into things, but they got no subtlety. When you'se dogs come around, everyone knows it. You'se all jump around like you're all hyped up on caffeine, knocking everything this way and that with your tails…" He suddenly notices that my tail has been docked. "Well, most of you'se, anyways. The point is, we cats are… sneaky. It's part of our nature. We blend into our surroundings, move as silent as the night, slip in and out of buildings without a single purr. There's a reason why they call thieves cat burglars, you know, and not dog burglars. Dogs just aren't built for this line of work."

He makes a good point. One of the reasons we dogs got a good rep for investigations in the first place is that our work is so visible, out in the open. And when a dog does something important, he can't keep it a secret. If nothing else, our tails give us away. Cats, on the other hand, can literally get away with murder and no one would be the wiser. They got the world's best poker faces. But I'm not going to give up on this. My buddy's life is too important for me to just sit around on my paws at home doing nothing.

"Antonio, I'll give you that. Most of my people are kind of oafish, built for nothing more than bouncing around in the backyard, barking at squirrels. But my breed is different. The humans specifically *designed* us for ferreting around. Or gophering around, if that's what's needed. We're small and fast, just like you cats. Granted I can't jump six feet in the air to clear a fence or hit a windowsill, but that's where you come in. Me, I'll just tag along in the background, staying out of your way. But I'll be there in a heartbeat anytime you need me."

He gives me the once-over, checking me out. "A Cairn Terrier, eh? Granted, you'se guys had a reputation for good field work in the old times, but nowadays you'se have all gone domestic. Lap dogs, if you know what I mean."

I feel like reaching out and snapping that smug look off his face. I've got four canines that are easily over an inch long, and I bet I could take him down long before those claws of his came into play. But once again, I remember why I'm here. This is not the time to play cat and dog with this guy.

"Actually, sir, I'm an Aussie, not a Cairn. People get us confused all the time. Same compact shape, same blonde hair and good looks. But unlike the Cairns, we Aussies were bred to be tough.

Fighters, not lovers. After all, Australia was founded by convicts, you know. By ruffians. It's in our blood."

Antonio gives me a speculative look. "Aussie, eh? Then why don't you have some kinda accent? You know, shrimp on the barbie, and all that?"

What an idiot. "Look, just because I'm an Aussie doesn't mean I was *born* there. I was born and raised right here in Chicago, same as you. I mean, you're a Maine Coot cat, but that doesn't mean you talk like you're from the northeast—"

"Maine *Coon* cat," Antonio interjects. That really seemed to tick him off. Fine. We can both play that little game. "But, okay, yer point is well taken. And yer right, even with my thirty pounds of solid muscle…" He holds up his arms and I can see the fat jiggling all the way down to his belly. "There may be some hounds out there on the mean streets that aren't easily intimidated, so you may come in handy after all. But I'm warning you, *cacciune*. One wrong move, if I so much as hear one little arf out of you, I'm gone and you'll never see me again until this thing is over. Got that?"

I don't really have a choice. It's a deal I have to take, or else I'm left with no option other than Sal over at the dog agency. And I'm under no illusions about what that would mean to the case. "Deal." I reach out my right front leg to tap paws and seal the agreement.

"By the way," Antonio asks, "I never really caught your name."

"Moose," I tell him, already steeling for his reaction. I get it every time.

"Moose!" Antonio breaks into a belly laugh, which, given the size of his belly, is a pretty spectacular sight. "Look at you! You're barely bigger than a Yorkie! What idiot decided to name you Moose?"

"It's from the Star Wars movie," I explain. "My humans thought I looked like an Ewok, and Moose was the name of…" Antonio is staring at me like he has no idea what I'm talking about, and I suddenly notice the time on the desk clock behind him. One crucial hour lost already. "Oh, what the heck, just ferget about it. Just drop it. We got bigger fish to fry right now. We need to hit the streets, and like yesterday. We've got a killer to catch, after all, and we've got less than two days left to catch him."

Hyde Park, 10:00 a.m.

So this is where it all went down, eh?" Antonio is examining the pavement closely, sniffing the ground, his whiskers lightly brushing the pavement in front of him. I spot a Pekingese eyeballing us warily from a window across the street. I can tell he's only seconds away from sounding the alarm, and then all hell is going to break loose on the street. We've got to get this wrapped up quickly and haul buns out of here.

I turn back to Antonio. "It was around dinner time last night. Killer and I live on the next street over. His back yard is right behind that little blue house over there." I point to the house just to the left of Pekingese. Antonio looks up briefly, checking it out, then returns to examining the faint blood stains. "I was over at his back fence, and we were just talking about this and that, guy things, you know, when all of a sudden we heard this loud screaming coming from over this way. I wasn't sure what it was at first, but Killer seemed to know instinctively that it was Penny. He cleared the fence in one jump and tore down the alley to get to her. I was just behind, running as fast as I could to keep up." I hold up a leg. "I mean, there are lots of advantages to being short, but speed is not one of them. Anyway, as I turned the corner onto the street I saw that Killer had just gotten to Penny. He muzzled her once or twice, trying to get her to respond, but she was pretty much gone by then. That's when all the humans started pouring out of their houses and spotted him, standing over her body with her blood on his mouth and nose. It didn't take them long to put two and two together and figure out what happened."

Antonio nods, taking it all in. "This Frenchie. We talkin' standard, mini or toy?"

"Standard, of course. Killer is a big guy."

"Sometimes that doesn't matter. But the thing is, you say you were with him the whole time. So you can vouch for him, you know he couldn't have been the killer."

"Yeah, but fat lot of good it does him. Try explaining all that to a human." I get another look at the Pekingese and decide we're pressing our luck. Time to hightail it out of here. "Antonio, things are going to start getting pretty noisy around here if we don't leave right now. Why don't we walk and talk?"

"Sure," Antonio agrees. "I've seen everything there is to see, anyway. Besides, the cleanup crew has already pretty much wiped out most of the evidence." He stands up and starts to slink away down the street, away from the Pekingese. I keep an eye out for any other trouble that might come our way.

"So, *Moose*." He says my name like it's some kind of a joke. But that's okay, I'm used to it. Get it all the time. "You were there on the scene. Did you see anything suspicious, anything at all that suggests who might have done this thing?"

"No. By the time I got to Killer and the body, I was completely wiped out from all the running, bent over, coughing and wheezing. I could barely see the nose in front of my face. Then suddenly the humans were all around us, screaming and pointing. Someone must have called the cops, because they were there almost immediately. One cop leaped out of his car with his gun already out, and if I hadn't jumped in front of Killer to shield him, he would have probably gotten shot and killed himself, and we'd have had two bodies to bury. As it was, Killer was pretty upset, snarling and snapping, wanting to know who had done this to Penny, and I guess the humans all took it the wrong way. Eventually I was able to get him calmed down and sitting quietly. Otherwise, they probably would have shot him regardless of what I did. But then Animal Control arrived on the scene, nabbed him and hauled him off in a paddy wagon to Southside."

We've made it to the corner, and I look up and see that my human already has a sign posted on the street light. This is no time to get picked up and locked inside, not when we're hot on the trail. We need to get out of the 'hood fast, get to someplace where I'm not so well known. "Hey, Antonio," I say, pointing to the sign.

He gets it immediately. "Yeah, I hear ya. But look, before we go, something I gotta understand. You say this dame Penny moved into the neighborhood only recently. When exactly did she get here, and where did she come from?"

"I don't know the whole story on that, Antonio. She was always pretty secretive about her past, like she was running from something. Or someone. And that may have something to do with her getting killed. Maybe her past finally caught up with her."

Antonio was looking back over his shoulder. Some humans were coming our way. Time to make like a tree and disappear. "Well, people don't get mauled like that for no reason. I mean, a drive-by I can see. But something this vicious, this sends a signal. Now we just need to find out who it was that needed to send it. And I got a good idea just where to start. Let's go."

The Bush, 12:30 p.m.

Where the heck are we?" I know we had moved south, along the lake, but these neighborhoods are all pretty foreign to me. When my humans take me along on car trips, it's usually into the city, or to one of the suburbs out west. Very rarely do we ever head south. There's probably a good reason for that. I'll have to remember to look into it, after Killer is free.

Antonio seems distracted as he answers. "We're on the South Side, heading for New Sullivan Elementary, in a neighborhood they call The Bush. I got a colleague here, a guy who's pretty savvy on the South Side packs that sometimes work yer part of town. Maybe he can give us some info on who might have been askin' around about a Frenchie lately, and who might have a rep for that particular style of — brutality."

Whoa. The South Side. If I'd known that was where we were heading, I might have stayed behind. I mean, I've heard the stories. A dog can get throated just for looking the wrong way on the South Side. "You sure this is a good idea?"

Antonio gives me a sideways look. "Only if we want to get to the bottom of who offed the Frenchie, and get your pal out of the slammer. But if you'se want to just pay me the rest of my fee and call the whole thing off…"

The fee. Twelve cans of tuna. Half up front, half when we're finished. I had a hard enough time getting my paws on the first six cans, and I have no idea where the rest of the tuna's gonna come from. But I'm keeping that to myself for now. "No, let's keep going. We're already past the worst of it. In for a kibble, in for a bit, as my pappy used to say." At least, I hoped we were past the worst of it.

New Sullivan looms ahead of us, three stories tall, almost all windows. Antonio points to the right and we circle around behind the school. "We going inside?" I ask.

"Nah, *mi paisan's* got a place near the playground. Easier than having to figure out how to get in and out, at least when the weather's nice. When it gets colder he has other arrangements. Look, I need you'se to be cool about this. Ike don't like strangers. Especially of the canine persuasion. Gets a little skittish."

"No, no, I get it. I'm cool." Actually, I'm not all that sure I am, but I don't think now is a good time to bring that up. Especially since I kind of forced Antonio to bring me along in the first place.

Tucked back behind the school is a small maintenance shed, locked to keep the kids out during the day and the tools and equipment in during the night. Did I mention the school is on the South Side? Where the shed backs up to the wall of the school, there's a small crack. Antonio slips through like it's nothing, but I have a tougher time. Probably because I'm so ripped. Not that I work out all that much. It's just good genes, I guess.

Eventually I manage to squeeze myself through the crack. There's a hole to my left that I can just barely clear, and then I'm inside the shed. It's almost jet black at first, but then my eyes begin to adjust to the darkness, and with the little bit of light sneaking in through the front door I can finally start to make out everything around me. Most of it is what you might imagine is in a maintenance shed — a mower, a couple of edgers, a gas can. And one big black cat. I mean, the biggest blackest cat I think I've ever seen. If I didn't know better, didn't know that we were deep in the heart of Chicago and not off in some South American jungle, I'd swear it might even be a black panther. The panther was speaking.

"What do you mean, bringin' dis filthy animal into my home?" The panther — I assume it must be Antonio's friend, Ike — is not happy, and he has something in his paw that looks extremely lethal. And it's pointed in my direction.

"Whoa, calm down, my friend." Antonio reaches out and presses the danger paw toward the ground. "Moose here is a client, and we're just trying to hunt down some information to get his buddy sprung from Southside lockup before he's put down. And we don't have much time. They're not gonna bring a vet in over the weekend, but Monday morning's comin' at us in a rush. So I gotta bend a few rules if we're gonna pull things together by then and save his life."

Ike doesn't look completely convinced. He flicks a paw in my direction. "You be sayin' he's a dawg, but he smells like a pig to me. You sure he's not a pig, mon? We don' need no pigs sniffin' around dese parts."

"Nah, he ain't no pig, Ike. Pigs, for all their faults, they're still pretty smart. This guy's as dumb as a goldfish."

Ike's slowly starting to come around. "Heh-heh, well, at least you can *eat* a goldfish, mon! But okay, if you vouch for him, ah'll look de other way. For today, though. Don't make it a regular thing, you know?"

"Sure thing, Ike." Antonio motions for me to sit on the floor, out of the way, then walks Ike through what we have learned about the case so far. It's not a long conversation.

"So, what ah'm gettin', mon, is you think this killin' might be the work of one of de South Side packs?"

"Well, not necessarily South Side, but that would be the group closest to where it all went down, so I'm takin' that as a safe bet."

"Yeah, ah'm with you on that. But de thing is, we haven't had any Frenchies around here for a long time. Poodles be too foo-foo for dese parts. So why would a local pack dawg go all that way north to go after some strange? That makes no sense, mon. I mean, someone gets mauled on the South Side, nobody cares. It's just one more, you know? But you start hittin' people outside de 'hood, den that just brings 'tention, de kind of 'tention people 'round here don' need."

"Exactly my thoughts, Ike. I just can't make heads or tails of it all."

I know Antonio had warned me to sit down and shut up, but hearing Ike use the word 'attention,' a sudden memory jumps up, something that might help pin down Penny's attacker. "Hey, I just remembered something Killer told me, something he mumbled as I was trying to get him calmed down." Antonio scowls at me, irritated, but Ike motions for me to continue. "As Killer raced to Penny's side, he said his attention was mostly on her, on getting to her in time. But as he was running her way, he looked down the street and thought he saw a big black dog racing from the scene. And he couldn't be sure, but he thought the dog was wearing some kind of dark red collar. Does that mean anything to you?"

Ike's face turns an even darker shade of black, if that is possible. "Ya, mon. Your talkin' de CCs. No mistakin' that, mon, it was de CCs, all right. An' that is very bad. Very bad indeed."

Antonio leaned in. "Who are the CCs, Ike? And how would they fit into any of this?" Antonio has apparently forgiven me for butting in, now that it appears I've broken open a new lead in the investigation.

Ike turns away from us, turns toward the light streaming in from the front door. My eyes have fully adjusted now, and I can see everything very clearly. Ike is scowling, deeply, and running a paw roughly across his face.

"De CCs are de Crimson Canines, a Doberman pack out of Calumet. They heavy in de drug trade, 'specially de cat crack bidness. Lots of money in de cat crack."

"Cat crack?" Antonio looks totally confused. "What are you talking about? Cats don't do drugs, other than a little catnip every now and then. And even that's pretty safe stuff. You can get it in the stores, humans grow it for you at home. But I've never heard of anything called cat crack."

"No, mon, that's just de street name. You know it by names like Whiskey Whiskas, Tiger Bites, that sort o' ding. Cats be goin' crazy on dat sheet."

Antonio finally seems to be catching on and is nodding his head, lost in thought. But I am just plain lost. "Antonio, what's he talking about?"

He pauses for a second, then looks up. "Moose, you know the old story about how cats are finicky eaters? About how humans can't get them to eat their food?" His accent is almost completely gone now, like he can't keep the act going and think at the same time.

"Yeah, I've heard of that, but I just thought it was an old pet's tale. I haven't been around a lot of cats, but the ones I have seen all look pretty well fed to me. And, frankly, as a dog, I can't imagine passing up a meal. I mean, my humans have even started putting my kibble in a stupid little bowl that I have to fight with every meal time just to get anything out. Who wouldn't just plow into their food?"

Antonio gives me that smirk again, all the while sharing a knowing look with Ike. "Okay, well, the thing is, the old story is true. We cats are actually pretty particular about what we eat, especially when the humans are trying to get us to eat junk that just isn't natural. Take Ike here. Most of what he eats he gets from hunting, plus some tidbits here and there from trash cans outside of the diners and grocers. All of it pretty delicious. And wet food, you know, the stuff from cans, wet food isn't all that bad once you get used to it. But that Cat Ciao crap, there's no way a cat is going to eat any of that, even if he's starving."

Ike butts in. "So some of de pet food peoples, they mix in de cat crack with de dry food. Cat crack makes de cats go crazy, an' they eat that sheet anyway."

"That's right," Antonio says. "It's just some kind of chemical they discovered that somehow affects a cat's brain, turns them all into addicts. It works with dogs, too, but with them it's not as strong. That's why you sometimes see dogs fighting with cats to get to their food. The kibble doesn't taste any better than their own food — in fact it probably tastes worse, since it wasn't designed for a dog — but the cat crack makes it irresistible."

Ike jumps in, nodding vigorously. "And de kitty treats, they even worse. Some got ten times as much crack, an' de cats follow their humans around all day long to get more crack."

I am totally floored by all this. Well, I was already on the floor, to be honest, but you get what I mean. "Wow. I had no idea that any of this was going on. Cat crack sounds like it's some pretty dangerous stuff. Why doesn't someone put a stop to it?"

"Who gonna stop it, mon?" Ike has turned back to face us, his face snarling with rage. "Humans do what they want with us, cats and dawgs. They get us addicted, den just sit back an' laff. They shine their little laser lights, make us go crazy, den just sit back an' giggle. It ain' right, mon. It ain' right."

Ike and Antonio have just opened me up to a world I never knew existed. Getting cats addicted to drugs, just to make it cheaper and easier to feed them. Maybe all those hippie naturalists riding around on their little bicycles were right after all. Now I kind of feel a little bad about chasing them. But, on second thought, nah.

Some of this still doesn't make much sense to me. "So Ike, how does all this fit in with the CCs? If the humans are handing out cat crack like there's no tomorrow, how is there a black market for the stuff?"

Antonio's the one to answer. "Supply doesn't always line up with demand, Moose. It's like food. Some cats get more food than they need, and some cats are starving to death. Particularly on the street. Ike here is an exception, mostly because he's a great hunter."

"I learn' de ways of de old country, mon," Ike explains.

Antonio nods. "And the humans aren't always ready and willing to dish out the treats, particularly when their cats get completely addicted and start to pester them all day long for more. Plus, the vets are starting to catch on to all of that, and are telling humans to lay off the drugs. But if you're addicted to the stuff, and your human suddenly starts holding out on you, going cold turkey just isn't an option. You gotta find a new source, a new dealer. And I guess that's where the CCs have carved themselves out a little business opportunity."

My head is swirling with all of this. I desperately need a chew stick right now, just to relax enough to take it all in. But chew sticks will just have to wait until after we solve the case, after we prove that Killer wasn't Penny's real killer.

"Ike, Antonio was right. You're obviously a total genius about all of this. So what I don't get is, why are you stuck out here hiding out in some rundown gardening shed? With a brain like yours, with your knowledge of how the world really works, you should be running things somewhere."

Ike and Antonio exchange another look. Antonio lays a paw on his friend's shoulder, softly. "I think this is just another one of those areas where things are different between dogs and cats. I mean, we all have our differences, our diversity. But with dogs, with all the hundreds of specialized breeds, you guys sort yourselves out along those lines. Dachshund versus Greyhound versus Malamute. But cats have a limited number of breeds, and even within those breeds there isn't a lot of variation. So where you guys may sometimes face discrimination based upon your breed — pit bulls, for example — the main source of discrimination among cats is based on their fur color. Specifically, the color black."

"No matter how smart a black cat is, we be treated like devils, by humans and even by udder cats," Ike explains.

"Think about all of the human superstitions regarding cats," Antonio explains. "It's bad luck if a black cat crosses your path. Witches are always shown cuddled up with black cats. Sailors think that if a black cat jumps on board a ship and then jumps off, the ship is doomed."

"An' in de shelters, de black cats never be taken. They always de las' to find homes, an' de first to be put down. But that startin' to change, now. Shelters be talkin' about how black cat lives matter, too. So mebbe things get better for us some day."

Man. It's pretty obvious I know next to nothing about cats. "Well, Ike, for what it's worth, I think you're pretty cool. In fact, when I first walked in here I thought you might be one of those famous jungle cats, like a prince, or a king. I — I know I'm just a dog, so my opinion doesn't mean all that much to you, but I'd be proud to call you my friend."

Ike's face softens, a slow smile starting to show, his teeth startlingly white against his indigo lips. At least I hope it's a smile. "Well, I don' know about havin' no dawg for a friend, but mebbe I was a little too quick in judgin' you earlier, my mon. Mebbe we all need to stop judgin' each udder so fast."

Antonio decides to change the subject, bringing us back to the reason we're here in the first place, Penny's murder. And his accent somehow seems to have returned. "So, the problem is, how did Penny somehow wind up in the middle of the crack trade? And what did she do that got her wacked?"

Ike is rubbing the back of his head with a paw. "That be de question, for sure. An' how did a poodle end up on de South Side widdout me knowing it? An' a standard at dat. That's a big dawg. No way to hide dat."

"Well, maybe we need to look into where she came from, before she showed up in my neighborhood a few months ago," I suggest.

"You got any ideas along those lines?" Antonio asks.

"Yeah, I know this Corgi, always has her nose close to the ground. And the rest of her, too, for that matter. Anyway, she seemed to be palling it up with Penny almost from day one. Maybe she knows something that can point us in the right direction."

"So it's all the way back to Hyde Park for us," Antonio says, raising one eyebrow.

I give him a sheepish look. "Sorry. I guess I should have thought of that sooner, while we were still there. Might have saved us some time. But all this private eye stuff is still pretty new to me."

"Dogs," Antonio mutters under his breath. "Always racing around before they stop to think." He turns back to face Ike. "Look, I've got to run down this lead, find out what this Corgi knows. In the meantime, would you mind asking around a little? See if you can chase down any rumors, or locate someone who may have seen the dame?"

"No problem, mon. I'll let you know first ting if I fin' out someting."

"Great. I'll owe you, my friend. Stay safe."

"You too, mon. An' about earlier, no problem wid your dawg friend. He's good peoples. For a dawg, you know."

Ike flashes me a bright smile, and I know that's a pretty big compliment coming from him. I return his grin with a quick wave, and Antonio and I head back north. I only hope Bella isn't trapped inside when we get there.

Hyde Park, 3:00 p.m.

We decide to take the alleyways this time. The Neighborhood Dog Watch is almost entirely focused on traffic in the front yards, plus that's where you're most likely to get spotted by humans at this time of day. And because I know all the dogs in the alley, I don't have to worry about setting off any alarms, even with a cat in tow, so the biggest problem is not getting distracted on the way to Bella's. Everyone naturally wants to hear the latest about Killer, and being his best friend, they think I have the latest poop on that subject. Which I guess I do, but it's not all that much, and I really don't have the time right now to share any gossip over the fence. So we just keep our noses to the ground and head as fast as we can to Bella's house.

We're in luck. Sometimes Bella's human — a friendly middle-aged lady who I think is getting a masters in something or other at the University of Chicago — forgets to unlock the doggie door before she races out for class in the morning, leaving Bella stranded inside. Pretty inexcusable, if you think about it, locking the door to the bathroom, but hey, it happens. Anyway, when we get to Bella's back fence and I let out my trademark 'arf,' she comes bounding out the door at full speed, barking furiously even though she knows it's me. She pulls up short, however, when she spots my companion.

"Uh, Moose, uh, what's the deal with the… you know… the…"

"The cat?" I finish the sentence for her. "Well, this is no regular tubby tabby, Bella." I hear a low growl from Antonio at that, but hey, I still owe him an insult or two from earlier. I continue the introductions. "This is a friend of mine, Antonio Gattograsso. He owns Felinvestigators, the feline detective agency, and he's helping me track down whoever murdered Penny. Antonio, this is Bella, the Corgi I told you about."

"Pleased ta meecha, ma'am," he says, sticking out a paw. Bella just looks at it, not exactly sure how to handle the situation. After an awkward moment, he drops the paw.

"Bella, you were pretty close to Penny, before…" It's still a little soon for all of us.

"You mean before Killer ripped her to shreds," Bella says, her eyes suddenly very dark.

I shake my head. "Look, you gotta believe me, Killer didn't have anything to do with it. I know you two weren't exactly friends—"

"Not after all those comments he kept making about my weight. I mean, I can't help it if I'm a little stocky. It's just how we Corgis are built. If my legs were longer you'd never think twice about it."

"R-i-g-h-t. Well, all that aside, I know for certain Killer didn't do it, because I was with him right here in this alley when it all went down."

Bella looks away. "Of course you'd stand up for him. You're his best friend. You'd say anything to get him off the hook. But I could see his muzzle from my front window, soaked with Penny's blood…" Bella looks like she's about to break down at this point. I glance over at Antonio for support.

He steps up closer to talk to Bella in a quiet voice. "Look, ma'am, I wasn't here, so I can't say for certain, but from what I've seen and heard today, I think Moose is telling the truth. Killer is innocent in all this." He pauses to let that soak in. "The thing is, if you're wrong, if someone else other than Killer wacked your friend, then I think you'd want us to find out who it was, and why he did it."

Bella is sniffling, and rubbing her nose with a front paw. She looks up at Antonio, then over at me, and finally nods her head. "Okay, fair enough. Just to be clear, I'm not changing my mind, and I hope the big brute gets what's coming to him, but just in case I'm wrong about this, which I'm not, mind you —"

"Thank you, Bella." I give her a gentle look. I know this is tough on her, and Corgis are all known to be overly emotional, and big worriers, but any lead we can get from her at this point is crucial. "Here's the deal. Earlier today we discovered that Penny had some kind of connection to a big drug ring down on the South Side. Do you know anything about that?"

"Penny? Drugs? Gosh no. She wouldn't even take her heartworm pills if they didn't shove them down her throat."

Antonio jumps in. "So you never heard her say anything about getting hooked up with cat crack? Maybe meeting a supplier from the South Side?"

"Cat crack?" Bella's eyes are wide open now, her forehead knotted with concern. "No, I don't even know what that is. Is it some kind of catnip?"

"No, not catnip," I tell her. "Something much, much worse." I decide to try a different tack. "Well, if she wasn't into drugs, maybe there was something else, something from her old neighborhood that had followed her here. Did she ever talk much about where she lived before her family moved here?"

Bella shakes her head, still a bit wary of all of this. "No, she always managed to change the subject whenever any of that ever came up. But I got the impression it was all pretty upscale. She may have been a model—"

I perk up at that. "You mean the dog shows? You think she was AKC registered?" That could be huge. I know a Pyrenees that is big into the shows. Maybe he might have seen her around.

"Yeah, she said her official name was Princess Penelope. That sure sounds like a model name to me."

Antonio is looking at me quizzically. I suddenly realize that, as a cat, he might not know much about the club scene. This is where my contribution to the investigation starts to become more obvious. "Antonio, the American Kennel Club is the official registry for pure bred dogs. If you want to raise dogs and adopt them out for money, the puppy's parents pretty much have to be AKC registered, to prove their bloodlines. And that's important for the dog shows, as well. You don't make the catwalk at the shows without having all the right papers in place."

He nods at me. "You're a pure bred Australian Terrier. Does that mean you're registered with the Club? Can you get us into one of the shows?"

"Nah, my bloodlines became irrelevant when they snipped off my kibbles and bits. But if Penny was active in modeling, there's a pretty good chance someone might know who she really is. And where she came from. I mean, the standard poodles are hard to miss at those shows, strutting around in their fancy French haircuts and all." I check the position of the sun in the sky. Still some time before dinner, when everyone heads indoors. "Look, if we hustle we might just make it over to one of my buddy's yard in time. He's been a show dog for years. If Penny was involved in any of the Chicago area dog shows, he'd know her for sure."

"Then let's get a move on." He turns to Bella. "Thanks for all your help, Bella. I know you're not convinced Killer is innocent, but if we can prove that he is, and we can bring the real dog that mauled your friend to justice, then in the end I think we'll all rest a little easier."

"And if we're going to make that happen, we'd better hustle," I suggest. "We're burning daylight right now." I reach through the fence to tap Bella lightly on the muzzle. "Thank you, Bella. I really appreciate it, and I know how tough all of this has been on you. But I'll swing back by early tomorrow. If you think of anything in the meantime, anything that might help us crack this case and find out why Penny was murdered, just let me know."

Bella sticks a paw out, stopping me. "Moose, a word please. In private." She nods toward Antonio.

"Oh, sure," I agree, and lean over toward Antonio. "Just give me a second with her. Might be something important."

"Okay, but make it quick. We're on a deadline, you know. Literally."

Antonio walks off down the alley, carefully avoiding stirring up trouble with any of my canine friends still eyeing him carefully from behind their fences. I turn back to speak with Belle. "So, you got something else for me you didn't feel like you could share in front of the cat?"

"Moose McGillicutty! Of all the bone-headed stunts you've pulled in your life, this one takes the steak!"

I've never seen her like this before, almost snarling at me she's so angry. "Wha — I don't—"

"Every time, Moose, every time! Puttin' on airs, like you're *somebody*. Like you're Mister Big Shot."

"Bella, it's not like that—"

"It's exactly like that. Your buddy Killer gets in trouble, and you decide you're the only one who can fix it. But it never works out the way you planned, does it Moose? Something always gets in the way, and it's never your fault. But now you've gone too far. Running off downtown, hiring some high-falutin' big dollar private eye. And just how do you plan to pay for that, Moose? You don't got no money. You don't got two bones to rub together. And you're foolin' yourself if you think I'm gonna to bail you out again—"

"Bella, you said yourself—"

"That I don't think Killer did it? Well, what did you expect me to say, Moose? You put me on the spot, got all up in my eyeteeth in front of some cat I've never seen before, and what did you expect? I *saw* him do it with my own two eyes. I *saw* him kill her."

"But Killer—"

"Penny is dead, and Killer is the dog who did it. Okay? End of story."

"So why did you—"

"Because arguing with you isn't gonna bring Penny back. And nothing we do or say out here is gonna make a hoot of difference as to what's gonna happen to Killer. He'll get the needle in two days, right as rain. And that's just what he deserves. So you need to get that into your thick skull right now, mister, and stop running around barking at squirrels like you're still some naive puppy. Grow up, Moose. Grow up before it's too late and nobody wants to deal with all your nonsense anymore. With all your stupid drama. Grow up while you still have friends like me who can pretend that they care."

I don't have anything to say to that. Don't now, haven't for a long, long time. Antonio is waiting for me at the end of the alley, tapping his foot. I have to go. I have to do this. For my friend. For myself. I turn my back on Bella and my past, and start walking toward my future.

"Moose!"

Bella's barks have always been pitched on the high side, but right now her voice is like a solid red stop sign springing up right in front of my face, stopping me dead in my tracks. Suddenly I can't feel my hind legs. Maybe she's changed her mind—

"It's time to put on your big boy collar, Moose," Bella warns me in a low voice, with an edge to her bark that I've never heard before and don't ever want to experience again. "You've been chewing on the furniture long enough. It's time you learned how to wear a leash for a change. Like the rest of us. Learn where the limits are."

A shiver runs through me, and I fight the urge to turn back, to give up. To put on the collar. And the leash. For her.

But I can't, not now. If I turn back now, if I give up on my best friend, if I let him die, knowing that he's innocent, how can I ever look at myself in a puddle again? Bella's words have my insides feeling like someone's put glass in my kibble, mostly because I know that they're true. Grow up, Moose.

Stop being a puppy. Don't always be the dog who lets everyone down. Everyone you know, everyone you love. Every time.

Antonio is waiting, and I pick up the pace, knowing that every second matters right now. A second too late is a second I'll regret the rest of my life. But still, I can't get her voice out of my mind. Out of my soul, troubled and confused as it is. Grow up.

That's all I've been trying to do, Bella, all this time. That's all I've ever been trying to do. The right thing. The big dog thing. The hard thing.

But I also know that the only way to make this right is to make it right. And Antonio is waiting for me at the end of the alley.

Little Italy, 4:30 p.m.

It's still broad daylight outside when we finally pull into Max's neighborhood, and, giving the street a quick up and down risk assessment, I suggest to Antonio that I think it's best if he stays well back and out of sight. Max is a known cat chaser, and I just can't guarantee Antonio's safety under the circumstances. He reluctantly agrees.

Max is a classic example of a Great Pyrenees, a breed also known as the Pyrenean Mountain Dog. At 150 pounds, he's on the upper side of the weight range, and his thick fur is almost snow white. More important, he's an old friend, and I can sure use one of those right about now.

Today Max is on guard duty, as he is every day. That's no big surprise — Great Pyrenees are always on guard duty. It's what they do best. Even though Max is a model, when he's not on the show circuit you can always find him sitting by the gate, his black eyes sunk back deep into his thick, wedge-shaped head, carefully watching every move you make. You can't sneak up on a Pyrenees. They sneak up on you.

"Hey, Max," I call out. "How's it hanging? Scare the beejesus out of any postal workers lately?"

"Hiya, Moose. Good to see ya. Gosh, you're sure roaming pretty far from home today. Everything okay?"

For a big dog, Max has a surprisingly squeaky little voice, like a young schoolgirl. Except, of course, when he lets out that booming bark of his. Then it's 150 pounds of sheer terror ripping right through your pants. I'm happy to say I've never had that particular voice directed my way, and I'm not quite sure how I'd react if I did.

"Nah, actually, I'm in a real bind and I need your help," I tell him. "Killer got himself arrested."

Max laughs at that. "Killer? Arrested? What did he do, accidentally wet somebody's leg or something?"

"No, Max, something really serious. He's accused of killing a Frenchie. His girlfriend at the time." I quickly walk Max through what we know about the case so far. “So the thing is, we need to get a positive ID on the girl, figure out where she was hanging out before she moved onto our street a few months ago. We think that might give us an angle on why the CCs wanted to kill her.”

“Sure, I gotcha.” Max gets quiet for a while, thinking back. “Yeah, I seem to remember this one chick a while back that fits your description almost to a T. She was a real hottie, won best of breed in almost every show she entered. Then something happened, and a year or so ago she started to slip, finishing second, then third, then out of the running entirely. Don’t really know why, but those shows can be really brutal. One little flaw and it’s all over for you, your career is over and done. I think I’m getting close to that point myself. The old hip dysplasia is starting to act up, and I’m no longer young enough to fight through it.”

“Gee, I’m really sorry to hear that, Max. You’ve been a great champion for a long time. I don’t think I’ve ever seen a Greater Pyrenees—”

"You're sweet to say that, Moose. But at some point it comes time to retire, to let the young pups have their chance. And this is a great fallback gig, hanging out here guarding the gate. It's like heaven for my people. Anyway, back to the Frenchie. I seem to recall that she lived with her humans out in Oak Park, before she dropped off the circuit completely about six months ago. I think that's where I'd start."

"Oak Park? That's quite a ways out there for a dog." Walking that far could take a day or more, and I just don't have that kind of time.

"Yeah, well, you can always grab the blue line or the green line out there. If you don't know how, ask that cat friend of yours, he'll tell you."

"Cat?" I look back, and even though I know where Antonio is hiding, I don't see a thing. Max is *really* good at this. I turn back to the gate, and catch Max grinning at me. "Okay, busted. I had to hire a private eye to help me out with this, and, well, Sal doesn't exactly have a very good track record these days."

"Don't have to explain things to me. Just get your butt out to Oak Park and find something that'll spring Killer. He's a good dog, even if he is a little dopey at times."

"Thanks, Max. And good luck with the arthritis."

"Sure thing. And give my best to the old neighborhood. It's nice out here, but it ain't the same since we moved."

I pat the gate lightly. "Yeah, I can't help but think none of this would a happened if you were still guarding the old street." Max motions with his muzzle and I see Antonio has finally stepped out into the open, signaling for me to get going. "Well, gotta run, big guy. Don't be a stranger."

"You too, Moose. You too. And, bring Bella around sometime if you get the chance. She still as bossy as ever?"

"You don't know the half of it, Max," I admit, thinking back on what she just laid on me. "Sometimes I wonder if she's worth it."

“Oh, she’s worth it, alright, Moose. She may bark a lot, but she seldom bites,” Max reminds me, grinning at me in that toothy way of his. “Maybe nips a little here and there, but never bites.”

I decide not to share with him how those little nips of hers just took a big chunk out of my own south side. And how that wasn’t the only part of me she really hurt. Not by a long shot.

Oak Park, 6:00 p.m.

I had never ridden the L before, at least not this way, jumping on and off like some kind of railroad tramp from the Great Depression. But once we're onboard, Antonio slinks away into a dark corner, out of sight, and I just hop up on a seat and sit there, smiling broadly, like I own the place. Yeah, I get plenty of stares, for sure, but these are all big city people with their own set of problems to deal with, and they don't want to add me to that list.

And I can't complain, it's all a pretty sweet setup. In no time we're trotting down Lake Street, looking for someone, anyone who can give us a solid lead on Penny. We decide to start our search at the dog park. We didn't bring any maps — I mean, we're a dog and cat, for gosh sakes, where we gonna put a map? — but you can hear the barks and growls at the park from miles away. In no time we're there, Antonio staying outside the fence for safety reasons, and me just hanging by the gate to slip through as soon as it opens.

As I enter the park, I check the place immediately for Frenchies. They're usually pretty easy to find, standing off to themselves, noses in the air, and this time I'm not disappointed. She's a little older, but manages to carry herself like she's still off doing the shows. Not bad if you go for that kind of thing. Me, I'm into chicks that are more down to earth. Like Bella.

I try to act casual as I stroll her way. Don't want to spook her, make her think I'm trying to make a play or something. I think about sniffing her, but at the last moment I decide she might take that the wrong way, getting too familiar too fast. You know how those Frenchies are, never say *tu* when you should be saying *vous*.

"Bonsoir," I tell her, testing the outer limits of my foreign language skills.

"Hmmph," she answers, turning slightly away and looking off in the distance where two dachshunds are busily chasing each other around a tree.

I decide to try a more direct tact. "Look, ma'am, I'm with the police. We're looking into a case involving a standard poodle who used to live around here, and I need to ask you a few questions."

She looks down her nose at me, clearly not convinced that I'm on the up and up. "Police dog? A puny little thing like you? Is this a joke?"

Okay, I get it. At fifteen pounds soaking wet, I'm no German Shepherd. But believe me, you don't want to be on my bad side. I gotta mouth full of teeth any Shepherd would be proud to show off. "I'm — I'm working undercover," I tell her. "Homicide. I'd show you my badge, but…" I indicate that there's just nowhere to pin a badge on me, which is good, because if they ever did it would probably hurt like the dickens.

I must have convinced her — or at least she's decided not to take a chance on impeding an official police dog investigation — because she lets out a long sigh and sits down, looking completely put out. "Whatever. Just ask me what you need to know and run along. I'm already late for my hair appointment."

There's no human standing anywhere nearby to haul her off to a groomer, but I'm not going to argue. Arguing with Frenchies is a hopeless cause — they just get mad and close up, shut you out. And right now I need her talking. "We're trying to run down some info on a certain standard poodle, goes by the name Penny, may also be using the name Princess Penelope. We think she may have been involved in the modeling trades, a real beauty, but was having some trouble in that area recently. Someone who knew her from the shows suggested she may have been living around here, at least up to around three or four months ago. Any of this ring a bell with you?"

Frenchie has gone from looking bored to totally alarmed. "Penny? And did you say you're from homicide? Oh my gosh! Is Penny okay? Is she—"

"I can't go into the specifics of an official investigation, ma'am," I tell her. "But we'd appreciate any information you could give us about her whereabouts. About who she tended to hang out with, what she did."

"I — I don't know what to say. Oh my gosh! Penny!"

She's totally hysterical at this point. Again, typical Frenchie. I need to get her settled down, and quick. Her human could show up at any moment, and she clearly has a bowl full of beans to spill on Penny. "Okay, ma'am, let's just start from the beginning. How long have you known Penny?"

"I — I've known her pretty much since she was a puppy, since she was adopted. Her human family was big into the club scene, and brought her around the shows when she was still very little, to get her used to the atmosphere, I guess. And she was a complete natural — you could tell right away that she was going to make something of herself, that she was going to be the poodle to beat for quite some time. It wasn't just her looks — she just had a kind of, how do you say, *je ne sais quoi*, you know?"

I don't know, in fact. I don't even know what jenny said kwa even means. Is that what the Frenchies call the woman scent? Anyway, I decide to move things along. I can see some people walking our way, and they look like just the sort of humans that would associate with a Frenchie.

"Right. A real knockout. She have any enemies you know of?"

"No, no, Penny was friends with everyone. A real charmer. I mean, some of the girls were a bit jealous at first, I mean who wouldn't be, but she managed to win them over in the end. Oh my gosh! In the end—"

She looks like she's about to break down, and the humans are getting closer. I need to wrap this interview up quickly, because she probably won't get another walkie until tomorrow evening, and by then it will all be too late.

"How about recently, before she moved. Did you notice any changes? Anyone new in her life? Anything about her habits that were different from before?"

She considers that. Out of the corner of my eye I can see the male human pulling a leash out of his coat pocket. "No, other than she was beginning to lose fairly steadily at the shows, which was new. That had her pretty down. I think she may have been starting to get desperate. Desperate to start winning again, to be a winner…"

The male human reaches down to clip the leash onto her collar. "That's a good girl, Foo Foo!" he says, condescendingly. "Come along now. You can visit with your little friend tomorrow."

She's leaving, my best line into Penny's past, and so far I got nothing. I call out to her one last time as she walks away. "Is there anything else, anything at all?"

She turns back, tugging hard at the leash. "Wait! There is someone, someone you need to talk to. Penny's astrologer, an Afghan just a few blocks from here, near Madison and Central. Ask for LuLu."

Then she's gone. And all I have is a name.

Madison and Central, 6:45 p.m.

I hook back up with Antonio and quickly fill him in on what little I've learned. With me taking the lead, we race south as fast as we can toward the intersection of West Madison and South Central Avenue. Toward a certain Afghan astrologer named LuLu.

Everyone's out for an end of the day walkie, so in theory it should have been pretty easy to ask around, to get the lowdown on LuLu's whereabouts. But humans tend to get a little nervous when strange dogs just trot up all alone without a leash attached to sniff butts and exchange idle conversation. And then there's the risk of that one Good Samaritan thinking he needs to collar the stray dog and return him to his owner. So Antonio and I decide we need to stick to the alleys again. Besides, dogs with outdoor privileges tend to know the score in their neighborhoods, not like lappies that only care about getting stroked and where their next meal is coming from.

For once we luck out. Apparently, LuLu's rather famous around these parts. Plus she's an outie, and her humans have long commutes in from the city, so there's a good chance we can get to her before she heads inside for the evening. Her back yard is all the way at the other end of the alley, so we hustle up. Every minute is critical now.

She's waiting for us patiently by the back gate, her long ash blonde tresses waving languidly along the side of her face and down past her jet black nose, her dark eyes watching us dreamily as we approach. She's wearing a woven linen collar the color of freshly picked Cabernet grapes — or is that Cabaret? Anyway, it's obviously not off the rack. She may be Afghan, but to me she looks like pure European royalty.

"And how can I halp you boys?" she asks.

She doesn't even bat an eye at Antonio. I guess, being a fortune teller, she can't afford to ever let on to being surprised by things. Even by a random cat showing up out of the blue asking questions.

I decide to take the lead on the questioning for now. I'm getting pretty good at this, if I must say so myself. Which I guess I just did. "Yes, well, I take it you're the famous LuLu, astrologer to the stars?"

She nods gently. "I'm not so sure about beink astrologer to the stars, but yas, the stars *are* my line of vork. I simply observe the silky skeins of the universe, see vere my client's lives are touched by the larger forces that shape our destinies..."

She trails off, and I hope she hasn't noticed Antonio rolling his eyes. "Well, great! You're just the person we've been looking for. As you probably know already, being like, able to see the future and all, my pal Antonio and I are trying to get some information about an old client of yours. A French poodle named Penny. And my name is Moose, by the way. But you probably already knew that."

"Ah, yas, Penny," she says. "A French poodle, indeed. But not just any poodle. A Princess." She starts to turn away. "I'm sorry for your troubles, but I'm afraid I'm just not inclined to discuss the private business of my clients vith strangers. I think you can appreciate my position. The ethics of my profession and all…"

Antonio decides to jump in at this point. I think he may be a bit ticked off by the fact that I've taken over the lead on everything so far. As you well know, cats are a little overly sensitive about protecting their territory. Although, to be fair, we dogs may have some issues in that department as well.

"Forgive me, madame, we are so sorry to intrude on your evening." Antonio has switched accents on me again, and now he's coming off like some English aristocrat. Or should I say, aristocat. "And while I fully understand your situation, I'm afraid I must inform you that the astrologer-client relationship between you and Miss Penny is no longer an issue. Miss Penny has… passed on to the other sphere, I'm sorry to say. And your duty to your client now has changed. You must help us find her killer."

A dark look passes across LuLu's face as she comes to terms with Antonio's news. "Yas, of course. The stars were always aligned against her. I told her that danger vas in her future. But she vouldn't listen. Always about the shows, how she vould do in the shows." LuLu pauses and leads us to a partially hidden section of chain link fence that a human at some point had cut a hole through. "Excuse my rudeness, darlinks. Please come in, make yourselves at home. And mind the edges of the fence. Rather sharp, I'm afraid. I *must* get someone to look into that…"

We crawl through the gap in the fence and sit down together as she arranges her long flowing hair and settles down in front of us, giving the ground a couple of turns just for good measure. I quickly take her through what we know.

"So, my Penny is now dead," she tells us, her long eyelashes drooping. "I vish I could say my powers could point me to her killer, but it doesn't really vork that way. The future, it is written in the stars, but the stars are much like the Milky Vay, very murky. Ve can see portents of the future, the general path that lies before someone, but the specifics of that path are lost in the shadows."

"Right. I understand completely." I shoot Antonio a sharp look, warning him to keep his thoughts to himself for now. But I agree. This dame's as crazy as a lizard with a sunstroke. No wonder they call her LuLu. "But here's the thing. If she *was* doing cat crack, she must have started using it a long time before she ever moved. No way she could have picked up a line on how to get her hands on that stuff in just the few short months she lived out our way. Not in my neighborhood, I would have known. Trust me, nobody barks in my neighborhood without me hearing about it. So that means her dealer must be from around these parts. If she got herself hooked into some kind of trouble, then that trouble must have started around here, and followed her east when she moved."

"Y-a-s, dahlink," LuLu murmurs, suddenly looking distant and distracted, like she can see ghosts or something floating around in front of her in the gathering gloom. Talking to her. Her lips move soundlessly for a few moments, then a stillness of some sort settles over her. "The trouble you are seeking. I see red. Red and black."

"The Crimson Canines!" I'm astounded. She really is… And then I suddenly remember that we already told her about the CC's. I sit back quietly, and pointedly try to avoid any eye contact with Antonio, who's staring daggers my way. I can almost hear what he's thinking right about now.

"Yas. The Cee Cees." LuLu waves a paw in front of her like she's cleaning mist off a mirror. "I see a name. So distant…" She leans forward, her focus apparently on something far away. "There is a dog. A black dog. Or brown. Very large."

"A Doberman?" I suggest, trying to remember if we had shared that part of the story with her or not.

"Yas. No." She wipes again at the empty air. "Maybe. Or maybe not a dog. A cat? Hmmm. So hard to know for sure… But… I see a name… F somethink…"

"Fido? Flapper? Festus?" I offer.

"Fish." A troubled look briefly crosses her face, then just as quickly disappears. "No, not fish. I see an eye. Just one eye. Bulging out, like a — fish eye." Suddenly she snaps back to reality and turns ever so slowly to gaze foggily in my direction. "Yas, that is it. The cat you are seeking, hiss name is Fisheye."

Mullin's Grocery, 7:55 p.m.

It's already dark, and most of the other pets in the neighborhood are already safely tucked inside for the evening. But the kind of cat Madame LuLu said she saw in her visions wouldn't exactly be the inside type. We headed straight to Mullin's Grocery, about a mile away. LuLu suggested she had seen flashes of the store in her vision. I think she knew which cat would have the answers about Penny's murder all along, and was just playing us for fools. At any rate, the information had cost me a high quality chew stick I had been saving for dinner.

The alley behind the grocery is poorly lit, and the ground is cluttered with empty boxes and assorted trash. Don't know why that would be, since there's a perfectly good dumpster pushed up against the back of the building with its lid hanging wide open. Humans, you know? Anyway, other than the trash, the alley's empty. I take a second to check under the dumpster, then stack a few boxes up and crawl to the top to take a look inside.

The smell is heavenly, a sweet mélange of rotting vegetables and tossed-out meat, and as I stick my head up over the edge I'm drooling already. Did I mention that LuLu messed up my carefully laid dinner plans? Anyway, there's a thin layer of trash lining the bottom, but nothing anywhere close to the size of a cat. I'm thinking about jumping inside for a quick snack when suddenly I feel a sharp blade being laid across the front of my throat.

"One fast move from you, *gato*, and *el perro* is gonna be breathin' from a new *boca*."

A quick glance to my left shows Antonio frozen in mid-step. Slowly he drops his back paw and holds out his two front paws, smiling. "Hey, *no problemo, hermano.*" Antonio takes a second hesitant step forward. "You must be Fisheye."

"Who wants to know?" the voice behind me asks. I can feel the knife bite a little tighter into my throat.

"We're friends of LuLu's. She told us we might find you around here. We just need to ask you a few questions, *capisce*?"

The blade relaxes a hair, and I finally catch a quick breath. Fisheye or whoever it is behind me hocks a fat loogie into the dumpster, just missing my right cheek. “That LuLu, shooting off her big mouth. *Boca loca*. She’s gonna wake up one day and find out that mouth has cost her her life, you know?”

I don’t think it would be all that helpful under the circumstances to explain to him that once you’re dead, you can’t wake up to find out anything. Best to just let sleeping dogs lie, if you know what I mean.

Fisheye speaks up again. “An’ she’s not the only one who’s loco, you know. You and the *perro* takin’ a mucho big risk sneakin’ around these parts at night. Lucky you ran into me, an’ not some crazy gangbanger, right?”

The knife at my throat pulls away a bit further and I look down to see it’s actually one of Fisheye’s front claws, filed down to a sharp edge. I shoot Antonio a quick warning look, but his eyes are locked onto Fisheye behind me.

"Right. Mighty lucky," Antonio agrees, nodding slightly. "So, Fisheye, about those questions—"

"I ain't answering no stinkin' questions from some fat *gato* and his scroungy *perro*." The blade is back at my throat again, and I'm praying Antonio knows what he's doing right about now.

"Heh heh, nice one, Fish." Antonio is grinning widely like that Cheshire dude, but his eyes are all business. "But just so's you know, I'm no alley cat you got here. You may have heard of me. The name's Fat Tony."

Fisheye lets out a low whistle and the claw drops away. "Whoa, you're Fat Tony? The guy who busted the Greyhound gang up in Evanston? Dat guy?"

"Yeah. In the flesh, you might say." Antonio jiggles his belly with his left paw. "And my amigo you've got there is Moose, a Cairn terrier from the city."

"Aussie," I correct him automatically. "Australian terrier." No one is listening.

I can feel Fisheye finally pulling back, his attention still locked on my partner. "So what would a high dollar detective like you be doin' hangin' around here? The barrio don' seem to be all that safe for a real fat cat like you."

"As I said, Fish. I'm looking for answers." Antonio starts walking our way, but he's still clearly got one eye devoted to Fisheye's knife hand. I stick one foot out cautiously, trying to find my way off the stack of boxes blindly in the dark. Slowly I try to ease away.

"What kind of answers?" Fisheye asks. "Don' nobody 'round here like to flap their *bocas* when there's trouble involved. Leads to a short life expectancy, if you catch my drift."

Antonio is nodding pretty much nonstop, and I'm starting to feel much better about our chances of getting out of here in one piece. Just then I step out into mid air and tumble free fall off the crates, banging roughly against the dumpster, then the crates, then finally landing upside down on my head, staring up at Fisheye. He looks like he's about to pounce on me at any moment, maybe jump down and gut me before Antonio can race to my rescue, but then he leans back and lets out a roaring belly laugh.

"Ha ha ha ha! That's one stupid little *perro* you've got dere! Look at the little *cabron*! Ha ha ha ha ha!"

Even Antonio is laughing at this point, and I'm feeling more than a little insulted, but then I realize that a rising knot on the back of my head sure beats a hole where my throat used to be, and I decide to just blow it off. "Very funny, guys," I venture, rolling off my head onto my side and trying to stand up, staggering a bit as I do. "Very funny. Glad I could give you a little show, there. Regular Ed Sullivan."

My head is now throbbing, and my right shoulder aches where it hit the dumpster, but otherwise I'm okay. I turn back to Fisheye. This is the first chance I've had to put a face to that voice, and oh what a face! I mean, generally speaking he looks pretty normal. For a cat. A smidge longer than I had expected, and well filled out, in a gym rat kind of way. His fur is black and gray, with hints of brown here and there. But his face! You can barely see where his sunken left eye is supposed to be, and an old scar running diagonally from the middle of his forehead down to just under his left ear suggests why. But what I can't help but stare at is his right eye, which is bulging out dangerously from its socket, and seems to be looking in every direction at once. Antonio's voice gives me an excuse to turn away before I make a complete jerk of myself.

"So Fish, as I was sayin', we're not askin' ya to narc out on anybody, but we have a situation here. My esteemed client Moose has a buddy who got falsely collared for offing his girlfriend, a French poodle. We got a little over a day left to find the real killer and bring him to justice, or else first thing Monday morning his friend gets a one-way ticket to the big dog pound in the sky. Or wherever it is dogs wind up. So we were just wondering if you might have picked up something on the street, something that might throw a little light on the situation."

Fisheye studies his paws for a moment. Finally, he seems to make up his mind about something and looks up, glancing quickly over at me, then back to Antonio. "Look, FT, I'm not sayin' I know nothing, okay, and I don't really cross paths much with the *perro* scene around these parts. I mean, I'm more into Calicos than French poodles, you know? More class and a whole lot less sass, if you catch my drift. But there was this one thing floatin' around a few months back—"

"That's right about the time she moved!" I can't keep my big mouth shut, and Antonio gives me a look that could melt an iceberg, so I clamp down and slink back into the shadows.

"What? You got a particular *senora* in mind?" Fisheye asks.

"Yeah," Antonio answers, tossing another visual knife in my direction. "Dog by the name of Penny, AKA Princess Penelope. A model by trade, big on the Kennel Club scene. Heard of her?"

"That's probably the dog I'm thinkin' of," Fisheye tells us, rubbing the side of his head absent-mindedly with his left paw. "Good looking beeatch, if yer into that sort of thing. Workin' it for all she was worth. But then she went deep and downhill fast on a drug we call kitty crack. Makes cats go all loco, like catnip but a hundred times worse. For dogs it works like a weight loss drug, and it's really taken off lately on the club circuit. Problem is, it's like the worse form of heroin, man. One or two hits and you're gone."

I share a quick look with my partner. Cat crack! "So what happened to her?" I ask.

"Don' really know for sure. She had a big problem, more than she could afford toward the end. She was gettin' older, you know, puttin' on a few pounds. The modeling gigs were startin' to fall off. So she tried the crack, to keep the fat at bay, thinkin' she could handle it. But it wound up handling her, instead. Big time. From what I understand, she picked up a jones she just couldn't afford, even with the modeling. And the gigs were still fallin' apart on her. That stuff makes you loco, you know, which was killing her in the talent competitions. So with no other way to pay for her daily fix, she did what too many *perros* do — she crossed over. Became a supplier, focusing on the club market. Other models who needed a little extra help with the LBs. The weight."

"So that's her connection to the CC's," I suggest, mostly thinking to myself.

"The CC's?" Fisheye looks at me like I just kissed his brother. "You think the CC's are involved in all this?"

"Makes sense," Antonio mumbles. "They're deep into the contraband trade, and we got some info earlier today tying her into the crack business. Have the CC's been making any moves into this area lately? Nailing down some dark, unwatched corners of the neighborhood?"

Fisheye scratches his chin with his razor claw. "I don' know, to be honest. I mainly focus on the second-tier commodities markets—" He points over his shoulder at the dumpster. "Lot of money to be made turning one man's trash into another man's treasure. And it's all mostly legal. Hard to make a case on a cat that's just recyclin' what yer throwin' away, you got me? But yeah, the CC's… it's possible. And the club scene is global, just the kind of grab they'd go for. So the Frenchie might live here, but the real business could be somewhere else entirely."

Antonio keeps pressing. "So word on the street — any idea why someone like the CC's might want to off her?"

"No idea." Fisheye sees something happening down the alley, and reaches over to check out something underneath a cardboard box next to the dumpster. "Look, I'd be happy to stay and flap our gums a little longer, but I have some local commerce issues to complete, if you know what I mean. Good luck to you guys, though." He pauses, rubbing an ear. "Say, you two don't really think you're going to try and take on the CC's, do ya? They're a bit out of your league, if you don' mind me sayin'."

Antonio gives him a quick sideways nod of his head and a wan smile. "Not too worried, *mi amico*. Handled the Evanston mob, didn't I?"

"But that's not the same thing, *hermano*," Fisheye shoots back. "The Greyhounds, they're Mafia. They got *rules*. But the Dobes ain't got no rules. You walk into there and *bam* you're like instant

Alpo. There won' be anything *left* to find floatin' in the river."

Antonio shrugs. "I'm a cat, Fish. I don't *walk* into anywhere. I'll get in, get what I want, then sneak back out, and the dogs will never know I was ever there."

"Yeah, well I hope yer right, FT. It's been a real honor meetin' ya, *jefe*. Wish I had more time to swap stories with you over a *cervesa* or *dos*."

"We'll have that time, Fish," Antonio promised, turning to leave. "More than enough time. And sooner rather than later."

"Yeah, well, however it turns out, *vaya con dios, mi amigos. Vaya con dios*."

I start to follow Antonio down the alley, then stop and turn back for a second. "Hey, Fisheye, if you don't mind my asking, how did you lose your eye?"

"Who said I lost it? I still have it, back in a jar at *mi casa*. Take it out for a walk every now and then, just like old times. *Sabe*?"

I don't sobby at all, but I have nothing to say to that, so I just shrug my shoulders and follow

Antonio back down the alley toward the big city. And a date with the CC's.

Navy Pier, 10:02 p.m.

Antonio tells me there are two places to look if you're trying to do a meet and greet with a CC — Joliet and the Navy Pier. The state prison won't do us much good tonight, and there's no way a dog or cat is going to get past all those prison guards, anyway, so we decide to focus on the pier. It's getting pretty late, so the trains back to the city are a little spotty, but as we slink onto the pier, hugging the shadows, a clock over a newsstand says it's just past ten. One day is almost toast already, and we still don't have any real answers as to who nailed the poodle.

It's Saturday night, and the joint is hopping with humans, all high on just about everything but life. Not only do we have to watch our own steps, we have to keep an extra eye out for the party crowd, stumbling around and threatening to pin us down with their size twelves. I notice Antonio has pulled in his tail and is keeping it tucked in close to his body. Being an Aussie, of course, I don't have that problem.

I lost my tail pretty much at birth. It's a religion thing, you wouldn't understand.

The pier is pretty well lit, but there are some dark corners tucked in here and there, the best places for a Doberman to hide out. Antonio says the CC's have been running the old snatch and bolt caper here lately, with a twist. Wait quietly in the shadows for some unsuspecting human to walk past, then one Dobe jumps out snarling and snapping while a second Dobe sneaks up from behind and snags the human's purse or wallet. It's all over in just a second or two, then the Dobes fade back into the shadows, and the humans have nothing to go on but a vague description of a dangerous dog and all those shiny sharp teeth.

Antonio waves a paw for me to follow, and we move further onto the pier, keeping a sharp eye out for any Dobes that might wander past. I spot a Golden Retriever and a few lappies, all out on late night walkies, but nothing even remotely resembling our targets. By the time we get to the end of the pier the crowd has pretty much petered out, just a few humans here and there swapping spit. Never have understood what they get out of all that. Me, I'm into lickies. Always a good way to keep up on my salt intake.

I have both ears up and rotating in every direction, trying to pick up on any stray conversations that might lead us to the CC's, when I catch a low guttural growl off to our right. I tap Antonio on his haunches and point in the general direction of the sound. "I think I've got something. Over there."

We move cautiously, knowing that one wrong move here could be our last. I pick up another sound, like something's being dragged along the ground just up ahead, and hold out a cautionary paw. Carefully, I ease my nose around a corner, sniffing, then risk a look. Nothing. As I turn back to consult with Antonio, suddenly something moves in the dark, something blacker than even the shadows, and then my head explodes right where I got my lump from earlier in the night, and everything else goes jet black.

Unknown Location

I wake up to find that I'm tied securely to a chair. Antonio is in a similar situation beside me, still passed out. I shake my head to clear out the cobwebs. It's not working.

"Hey Ralfie, look wut just woke up."

My head is pounding like someone's trying to drive a railroad spike between my eyes, and my mouth tastes like a bum's armpit after an all night bender. As the fog starts to lift from my eyes, I can just make out the outlines of two of the biggest, meanest looking dogs I have ever seen. Whatever light is in the room is coming from an open doorway behind them. One of the dogs has some sort of long black rod he keeps thumping into the palm of his left paw, a sound that isn't helping my head one bit.

"I don' know why wes have to go to all this bother, Fang. Tyin 'em up an' all. Seems like a waste."

"Yeah, well, you know wut Boss Dawg told us. Everythin' hast to be done in de right order. First we get ‘em to spill dere guts, then we get to spill dere guts.”

“I hears ya. But wut we gonna lern from some dumb Yorkie and a lousy cat, anyway? Just a big waste of time, I tell ya.”

I start to correct him about the Yorkie bit, but the effort makes my head feel like it’s about to split in two, and on second thought it seems that keeping my mouth shut right now might be the best move I have.

One of the big dogs is speaking again. “Well, they better start yipping soon, ‘cause I’m hungry. And that cat looks like he’s got a good load of fat on ‘em, ya know?”

“Dat cat is *mine*, Ralfie. I bagged him myself. You git the little runt.”

“Tell you wut, Fang, why don’t we just split it. Plenty of meat to go around. And you’se can have the Yorkie to yerself fer a little whet yer whistle, eh?”

I’m not liking the way this is going, and if I don’t do something pretty quick it looks like I’ll be beating Killer to the great boneyard in the sky sooner rather than later. Antonio is still lights out beside me, so he's not going to be any help. I figure, what the heck, given the dire situation I might as well go all in on this one. They're barking back and forth, not paying no nevermind to me, so I rattle my chair to get their attention. "I'll have you know I'm an Australian Terrier, you idiots," I tell them.

The dog called Fang looks my way and smiles. His canine tooth on the upper left side is covered completely in glittering 14 carat gold with one large brilliant-cut diamond set dead in the middle. "Well, well. Looks like Yorkie's got an att-ude, Ralfie."

Ralfie leans forward, showing his impressive canines as well. "Jus' makes it more delicious goin' down, I say."

It's clear these guys are just a pair of stooges, but I need to get their minds off their stomachs toot sweet before I become a midnight snack. They mentioned something about a boss something or other. Boss dog? Yeah, that's it. "All I know is one of you two idjets better untie me before boss dog gets here or he'll have your hide fer sure."

Ralfie and Fang share a panicked look between them. “You know Boss Dawg?” Ralfie asks.

“Yeah, you bonehead,” I tell him. “Why else you think I got this cat? Caught him askin’ around about the poodle job, thought the boss might want to find out why.”

My little lie seems to have done the trick. Fang is eyeballing Antonio with a new respect. “Hey, Ralfie, how’d dis cat find out about de double cross, ‘bout how dat dame took a powder on us? I tought dat was need ja know information. We got some kinda leak in de organization?”

Fang looks like he’s about ready to untie me, but Ralfie stops him with a quick paw to his shoulder. “Hold on a minute, Fang. Maybe the runt’s on the up and up, or maybe he’s just feeding us a line. Why don’t we keep him and the cat under wraps until we can find out which way it goes.” He shrugs toward the open doorway. “You keep watch out there, make sure no one comes lookin’ fer ‘em. I’ll go back to the wharves to fetch the Boss.”

Fang hesitates a second, like he's thinking it over, but it's clear to me Ralfie has the upper paw in all this, and in a minute or so the door is shutting behind them with a loud click and I'm left tied to a chair in the dark. I turn to try and wake up Antonio, see if he has any ideas on how to get us out of here, but he's gone! "Antonio!" I call out loudly, hoping he can hear me, that he hasn't gotten himself trapped behind a closed door in some other room, when suddenly I feel a sharp hiss in my right ear.

"Hush, you fool! And stop wiggling so much. It's hard enough to untie you as it is."

"Antonio!" I whisper. "How did you…"

"Get free? Ha! Those foolish canines, thinking they could keep a cat tied up somewhere. Never happened once in the history of the world, for sure ain't gonna happen here. You can't even keep a collar on a cat less he wants it on."

In seconds I feel the ropes go slack on my wrists and I immediately bend over and go to work on my legs. I'm not making any progress when Antonio comes around and with an outstretched claw and some kind of twist of the wrist I'm free. I shake my paws for a few seconds to work the circulation back into them while Antonio moves over to examine the door.

"Antonio, I thought you were out cold for sure."

"Yeah, that's what I wanted them to think, but I was watchin' them the whole time, lookin' for an angle on how to spring us out of here. Good job, by the way, buyin' us some time. Might make a detective out of you yet."

The room was almost pitch black, but Antonio's pupils were fully flared and he was carefully running his whiskers along the door frame, checking for weaknesses. "Okay, Moose, this looks like our only way out. They got it locked — don't know why they bothered, since we were both tied up — but there's never been a lock a cat couldn't pick when he sets his mind to it."

Antonio holds up his right paw and immediately two claws pop into view. He glances my way. "A little room, if you don't mind? This is sensitive work."

I push back a step or so and try to follow what he's doing in the meager light drifting in from around the door. He sticks his claws into the lock, probing. After a few minutes he pops out a third claw on his left hand, and works his paws in unison on the lock. Finally I hear a loud click that sounds almost like a gun going off in the quiet room, and I jump back and knock over one of the chairs.

"Quiet!" Antonio whispers. "They're gonna hear us for sure, the way you keep banging around in here!"

"Sorry," I mumble back, but Antonio has already forgotten me and is working at opening the door. A wide crack slowly appears and he peeks out.

"Looks like the coast is clear." He turns his head ever so slightly in my direction. "Okay, Moose, we got one chance at this, and we better make it good. If anyone's waiting out there for us, with those short legs of yours they'll nab you for sure. So here's the deal. You hang back for a second, let me take the lead. Soon as you hear me hiss, you hit the ground running like your tail is on fire, got me?"

"What about you, Antonio? Those are big dogs out there. How are you going to escape?"

"Don't worry about me. A cat ain't worth the fur he's wrapped in if he can't escape the clutches of some stupid cur. Thing is, you pick a direction and just keep going. I'll meet up with you when we're in the clear. *Capisce*?"

I'm not really capeeshing anything at this point, but any plan's better than what I can come up with, so I just nod my head and kneel down in a crouching position, ready to hightail it out of here as soon as I get the signal. Antonio opens the door just a tad more and somehow manages to slip through the tiny crack to the outside. In seconds I hear the sounds of somebody or somebodies leaping to their paws and barking like it's Christmas morning and someone's left a roast untended on the kitchen counter. My ears are perked forward, sonar fully engaged, and then I hear it. A hiss, unmistakable.

As I bolt through the door, everything is in chaos. Dobermans are running every which way, barking. They're all mostly looking up, which means they're not watching where they're running, and two Dobes collide right in front of me. I dodge to the left and instantly see my opening. Two large stacks of boxes, with a crack just my size between them and a some kind of light glowing well down the street. I take off toward it at full tilt, aiming for the crack, but a Dobe off to my right has spotted me and is now making chase. I hit the crack just ahead of him and hear with no small satisfaction the sound he makes slamming into the boxes. The tower starts to collapse onto both of us, but somehow I barely make it free and leap into the open street just as the two stacks cascade down behind me and settle like a solid concrete wall right onto the back of my pursuer. Another Dobe is onto me by now and has rounded the pile of boxes just as I hit a line of parked cars. Staying under the cars and running like my life depends on it — which, quite frankly, it does — I manage to stay just out of reach of his snapping jowls. But up ahead I can see that I'm rapidly running out of cars. If I burst out into the open road he'll have me for sure, but if I try to hide under the cars, it's just a matter of time before his buddies catch up and corner me. Either way I know my goose is cooked. Which is, by the way, how I prefer my goose. I've almost given up hope when suddenly I hear a loud thunking sound, and the Dobe immediately drops to his knees. I redouble my speed and shoot out from underneath the last car. I risk a quick look behind me, but the Dobe is lying in the middle of the road, his tongue hanging from his mouth, a large beer bottle lying broken in half beside him.

"This way, Moose!" shouts Antonio as he flies off the car behind me and lands lightly and already at full speed just off to my right. He cuts across me toward an alleyway to our left, dodging bags of trash and other things I can't quite make out, and I'm doing everything I can to keep up. Finally we burst out of the alley and onto another street. Antonio spots an open doorway and heads for it. We duck inside, he pushes the door almost shut, and we both collapse onto the ground, fully exhausted and completely out of breath.

"What is this place?" I ask when I can finally spare the oxygen.

"Warehouse district, I think," Antonio answers. "Lots of abandoned buildings, perfect place for a hideout. Or a headquarters."

"Those were some pretty slick moves back there, Antonio. That you with the beer bottle?"

"Yeah, you were running out of room and time, so I figured I had to do something," he tells me. "Glad it worked out, but I only had one shot at him, and throwing a beer bottle with no opposable thumbs is a tricky piece of work, I'll tell ya."

"Well, thanks for that. I owe you big time, buddy. You saved my life."

"We'll have time enough to worry about that later. The thing is, while I don't think I'd want to try our luck like that again, getting captured actually worked out in our favor." He moves back to the door to peek outside. "Looks like we must have lost 'em. I imagine they'll all scurry around for a little longer, like a bunch of ants when their hill gets knocked over, but then they'll eventually give up the chase and head back to their HQ. So this gives us a great opportunity to find out what really happened to the poodle. We got some idea why, but we still need to figure out the who."

"How's that?" I ask. "We're at a dead end, now. Surely you're not suggesting we go poking around with those Dobermans again. That would be total suicide."

"That's exactly what I'm suggesting, Moose. You remember back when you mentioned Penny to them? They reacted like they'd just seen a ghost. Plus, the last thing they'll be expecting right now is for us to head back right smack dab into the middle of their operation. Also, we know that the Dobe named Ralfie headed over to the Navy Pier to bring back his boss, who had to be in on the murder himself. So if we can manage to sneak back over there where we can get some eyes and ears on what's going on, maybe we can learn something useful. As you say, it's either that, or we got nothing. And I'd hate to think we almost became din-din for those mutts for nothing."

Once again, I think the plan stinks, but I got nothing. And if the tables were turned, Killer wouldn't hesitate to stick his neck out for me. It's just that, well, a pit bull's got a much sturdier neck than I do, if you know what I mean. Anyway, I'm out of options, so I look over at Antonio and nod. "I guess this whole thing's been one big case of jumping out of the frying pan just to fall right back into the frying pan. I only wish this didn't sound like such a really bad idea, Antonio. And, by the way, I don't have to remind you that we dogs get just one life. When we're dead we're dead. We don't get to keep eight spares just sittin' around, like some folks I know."

Antonio is already opening the door and heading outside. He stops and glances back. "If there's one thing I've learned over the years, Moose, it's all about having the right balance in your life. Whatever you do, whatever life throws at you, you gotta remember to always land on your feet."

I remember all the times I accidentally fell off the couch and onto my head during much easier times, and suddenly I'm not feeling all that good about any of this. Maybe Bella was right, after all. Maybe I'm just not cut out for this hero thing.

CC HQ, Well Past Midnight

Somehow we've managed to snake our way past all the sentries and have finally staked out a position on the roof just above what appears to be the CC's headquarters. Dobermans are still racing around like crazy, apparently trying to figure out what hole we disappeared into. One Dobe in particular is nursing a bad cut on the back of his head. A cut roughly in the distinct shape of the bottom of a beer bottle.

Antonio and I have split up our assignments. I have my ears trained on the action below, while he has his see-in-the-dark feline eyes carefully tracking everyone's comings and goings from the main door into the HQ.

Suddenly there's a big commotion just down the street, and the biggest dog I think I've ever seen comes strutting down the middle of the road straight toward us, with a phalanx of lesser Dobermans following along behind him. My guess is the big fella is Boss Dog, and that's a guess I'd wager Milky Bones on.

"Who's in charge here?" When Boss Dog barks out his orders, everyone turns on a dime and stands at attention. "What's happened? Where's Fang?"

Fang has been hiding inside a large cluster of other Dobes and reluctantly steps forward, hanging his head.

"Report, soldier!"

Fang seems to be struggling with raising his head to face his commander. "You see, sir," he stammers.

"Stand at attention when you speak to me, soldier!" Boss Dog bellows in his face.

"Yes sir, sir!" Fang stands up ramrod straight, his eyes still staring off into the distance, carefully avoiding eye contact with his Boss.

"Where are the intruders tied up, soldier? I want to see them right away!"

"Well, you see, sir," Fang answers, weakly. "They kinda sorta… escaped." His voice trails off to a whisper as he struggles to get out that last word.

"Escaped!" The word comes loaded with a hail of spittle that flies across the space between them and coats Fang's hangdog face, dripping down slowly onto the ground. "You let our prisoners escape? What kind of — how in the world did you—" Boss Dog looks around at the swarm of Dobermans scattered all around him, each of them carefully examining their hind paws. He turns back to face Fang, furious. "Are you telling me, soldier, that you had a *cat* and a *Yorkie* tied up in a locked room and you let them *escape*?"

I want to shout out that I'm not a *Yorkie*, but Antonio puts a steadying hand on my shoulder and I sit back down.

"Yes sir. That's exactly what happened, sir. No excuses." Fang is wearing a beaten expression, completely deflated.

Boss Dog turns to speak to another Doberman, one of the group that had accompanied him on the walk back from the Navy Pier. "You! Take care of this mangy cur. You know what to do. And somebody please tell me how in the world two scroungy house pets could possibly bust out of my own headquarters and nobody laid a single paw on them in the process!"

We watch as Fang is led off to jail and another dog steps up to brief his commander on our escape. I have to admit I'm kind of enjoying watching all this. I've never seen a Doberman actually get red in the face before.

Finally, the boss summons Ralfie for a quick debrief on what he learned about us before he headed out to the pier.

"Yes, Boss, the Yorkie said he caught the cat poking around into what was going on with that two-timing poodle Fang offed—"

That's it! That's the proof we need! It was Fang who killed Penny! I turn and look over at Antonio with glee, but the look I get back in return stops me cold.

"What's wrong, Antonio? We found him! Now we just need to turn him over to the humans."

But Antonio isn't listening to me. He's just staring down at the crowd below us. Finally, he raises one paw and points. Off to one side, roughly halfway between the Boss Dog and the front doorway to the headquarters, Fang is lying in a rapidly spreading pool of his own blood.

"Dead men tell no tales," Antonio mutters. "And that goes for dead dogs, too."

Fat Tony's Office, Sunrise

We're back at Antonio's office. I'm sitting quietly in front of the desk while he stares out the window, sipping on a cup of coffee. I don't know how he can stand the stuff — I got a mouthful once and believe me, it'll be my last.

Finally, I can't stand the suspense any longer. I gotta say something.

"So what are we gonna do now, Antonio? How are we gonna get the humans to spring Killer, now that the real killer is dead?"

Antonio puts his cup down and turns away from the window. "Theoretically, we might be able to get one of the other Dobermans to finger him. But that's just theory, and Dobes don't actually have any fingers. So there's that."

The sun is starting to rise, leaving Antonio just a shadowy outline to me. Reminding me of our first meeting in this office, a little less than a day ago.

"But we can't just give up," I protest. "There's gotta be some way we can save Killer, some way to prove that he's innocent."

"Even under the best of circumstances, that would be pretty difficult," Antonio suggests. By now, he's completely abandoned the accent. If anything, he sounds like a TV weatherman, talking about fronts and backs and all that kind of stuff. "After all, Moose," he continues, "we don't speak or write human. We'd have to hunt down a parrot somewhere, and even then somehow convince it to help us out. And you know how those featherbrains are. Every one of them's a Pollyanna. All they ever seem to care about is getting their beaks on a new cracker. Never about what anyone else needs."

"But even saying we could find us this beneficent bird, how are we going to convince him we're right, that it was Fang who killed Penny?" I ask. "And we're not even all that sure why he did it in the first place. Without motive, and without a live Doberman to tie to the crime scene, it's just our word against the humans."

"And humans almost always trust their own kind first. It's the law of the jungle, and it's their jungle we're playing in." Antonio taps a paw lightly on his desk. "But maybe we're playing this all wrong, Moose. Now that I think about it, proving Killer's innocence was kind of a fool's errand all along."

I can't believe what I'm hearing, that the famous Fat Tony is giving up on me. "But we gotta try, dangit! We still got a day. Maybe something will turn up. You can't just quit!"

"Who said anything about quitting?" Antonio has turned a little sideways to me, and from the light slanting in through the window I think I can see a small smile blossoming on his face. "Fat Tony never *quits*, Moose, and I'm not about to start that nonsense now. I'm just saying, maybe we came at this whole thing from the wrong angle. Maybe we don't need to prove Killer's innocent after all."

I'm not following where he's going with this at all. "But — but — if he's not innocent, then they're gonna put him down. They don't cut killer canines any slack at all. He won't even get a trial!"

Antonio has turned back, facing me now, and is leaning forward, resting both front paws on his desk. "The thing is, Moose, you can't stick the needle into someone who ain't there. Maybe we can't save your friend by convincing the humans he's innocent. But that doesn't mean we can't save him, anyway."

"What are you saying?" I ask, completely confused.

"I'm saying, if he can't walk out of prison a free dog, at least he can sneak out of prison with a price on his head. The price humans always place on dogs that manage to pull off a prison break."

Antonio starts grabbing at things like he's about to leave. "Look, you stay here for a bit," he tells me. "I gotta go see a man about a dog."

"See a man?" I ask. "What man? What dog?"

"It's just a sayin'," Antonio explains, mumbling to himself as he heads out the door. "Dogs! Sheesh! Uneducated flea bitten…"

Fat Tony's Office, 7:30 a.m.

He slinks into the room so quietly I never even heard him open the front door. Antonio scoots around me unceremoniously and leans heavily against the desk. He's looking straight at me, but his mind seems elsewhere.

"What did you find out, partner?" I've been chewing on my nails ever since he left. All the inaction and sitting round doing nothing is killing me inside. "Any ideas on how to get him out?"

"Maybe," Antonio drawls, moving over to study an old, yellowed map of the city of Chicago hanging on a side wall of the office. He pushes a chair directly beneath the map, then jumps up onto it, now staring at it at eye level.

"I got a friend runs the sewers," he says, pointing a paw at a spot somewhere on the south side of the city. "He says there's a main line that used to run through here, just under where the Southside Prison was constructed, back in the 30's. Abandoned, now, but still accessible, if you know where to look. Used to be home to several speakeasies, back during Prohibition days. Place where a fella could get a little off-the-books libation, if you know what I mean. Now all the furniture and stuff is still down there, but it's all been completely forgotten. By the humans, at least. And that's gonna work in our favor."

"A sewer?" I'm not at all sure about this plan. I mean, working our way through dirty alleys and filthy streets is one thing, but I'm not the kind of dog that goes rolling in somebody else's poop. Smell it, maybe, but not roll around in it. That's why God made pigs.

"Yeah," Antonio answers, still studying the map. "It's perfect. That is, assuming we can figure out where to set the explosives."

"*Explosives*? What do you mean, *explosives*?" Okay, this plan has officially gone from bad to worse. Now we're talking about blowing poop up. And when that stuff hits the fan, there's no telling where it's going to land.

Antonio looks back at me, smiling like he's enjoying the moment, enjoying the look I know is plastered all over my face right about now. "Don't you worry about it, little fella. I got this covered. Got professionals on it, people who know what they're doin'. Now we just gotta iron out two or three little wrinkles, and by close of bizness tonight, Killer will drop out of sight for good. Right under the humans' skinny little noses."

All I can think about right now is sewers and noses, which is not a terrific combination, if you ask me. But Antonio mentioned wrinkles, so I wrinkle up my muzzle, trying not to think about the smell, and wuff to get his attention.

"You said there are still some kinks in the plan we gotta work out. What do you got in mind?"

Antonio drops down from the map and saunters over to where I'm squatting in a leather chair just in front of the big oak desk. He examines his left paw for a moment, licks it, then washes the left side of his face. I get the impression he's stalling, but as usual I sit and wait patiently for him to continue.

Finally he looks up. “My contact says there ain’t no manhole in that stretch of the sewer that hasn’t already been sealed up or covered over, so’s if we want some kind of escape tunnel from the sewer to whatever’s overhead, we’ll have to make one. That’s where the explosives come in. We’re gonna need to blow a hole in the top of the sewer and out into the prison yard, something big enough that your friend the pit bull can squeeze through.”

“But that’s really dangerous!” I complain. “What if the explosive goes off in the wrong spot, and somebody up top gets hurt?” By somebody, I mean some dog, of course. By my reckoning, the humans took on that risk when they built the prison in the first place.

“Which is why we’re heading south toward the prison right now,” Antonio explains, already trotting toward the door. “I think I’ve got an idea for how we can triangularate the right location, so we can set the explosive in just the right spot before we blow it.”

I got no idea what he means by strangulating the right location, but that's not the word that's got my mind in a tizzy at the moment. "You keep talking about the explosives, Antonio," I say to his back as the door slams behind me, leaving us walking briskly down the hall. "Where we gonna get some explosives?"

"Just a minor detail," he explains, already halfway down the hall. "Just leave that to me, and we'll tackle all that later on this morning. Right now, we gotta work out detail number one. Where exactly we can place the dynamite in the first place. I don't know if you've ever worked with the stuff, but it's kind of a delicate operation, like baking a mousse. One false move and—" He makes a motion of bringing his paws together for a moment and then spreading them out quickly and dramatically. I don't really know why he's thinking I need to be baked in the first place, but I've got a queasy feeling in the bottom of my gut that would have me heaving my kibbles right now if I had any to lose. Once again I'm laying my life and the life of my best buddy in this cat's mangy feline paws, and I just hope against hope that I'm making the right decision. There's a reason dogs never really trust our little cat friends, you know. And thousands of years of evolution establishing those natural instincts just can't be all wrong.

The L, 8:00 a.m.

Antonio is catching me up on his ideas as we hop the L for the south side, heading for Killer's prison cell.

"So, Moose, we still need to work out the details, but assuming we can spring him somehow, your friend is probably going to end up in PETSEC."

"Pet sick? Never heard of it. That some kind of veterinary hospital?"

Antonio runs a hand roughly between his ears. "Not pet sick, you dunce. PETSEC, the Pet Trauma and Security program. And yeah, there's a good reason you haven't heard of it. PETSEC is like a pet's version of what the humans call a witness protection program, WITSEC, a way of making people disappear when someone's out gunning for 'em." Antonio motions to me to get ready to hop off. We've apparently come to the end of the line for this particular train. "So, say a dog is wanted, like your friend Killer. Or say he's being mistreated, beaten or starved by his master, chained up out back, and nobody steps in to save him. Well, if the humans won't protect him, somebody has to. That's where PETSEC comes into play."

We're now on the platform and heading for our last train, dodging clumps of humans staggering along the platform like zombies, barely noticing as we weave our way in and out among their feet. "Okay, I got that part, Antonio, but if a dog has a record, like Killer, then eventually won't they just capture him again? And then we're back to square one on all of this."

"Nah, that's the beauty of it." We manage to hop onto the train just as the doors start to close and grab a spot under a vacant bench seat. "You see, Moose, there are only two ways humans can identify their pets, assuming those pets don't want to be identified. I mean, obviously, if a dog waddles up to its human wagging its tail and licking the human's face, that's generally a good indication that they've got the right dog. But what if a dog acts all aloof, like we cats do? By the way, it's something we train for from the time we're kittens."

"Can't they just check the dog tags?" I ask.

"Sure, if the dog's wearing any. But more and more these humans are having their pets chipped. Used to have them tattooed, but now the chips are the going thing. Lets a human run a magic wand over a dog or cat's butt and a number comes back that tells him which specific human belongs to the pet."

"Kind of like sniffin' butts," I suggest.

"Yeah, something like that. But a lot more hygienic." Antonio is shaking his head and giving me that superior cat look he's been wearing most of the time I've known him, and I can almost hear what he's thinking. Something about dogs and how he thinks we're all disgusting. But hey, unless you're willing to try something, unless you're willing to walk in another pets shoes — assuming we have shoes, which ain't all that common — then you got little room to criticize. In my humble canine opinion.

But Antonio is mumbling again, so I listen up. "Anyway, the key to a successful PETSEC intervention is to lose the tags and the chip. That way, every dog looks for all intents and purposes like any other dog of its breed."

"But that's stupid, Antonio," I object. "No two dogs look alike. I can tell my friends from strangers in a barkbeat."

"Yep, you'd be right, to some extent. And I'm the same way about cats. But it doesn't work out that way between species. And that's especially true when it comes to humans — they often even have problems telling each other apart. I had one case out in the western suburbs, stupid humans were certain they had the right guy, thought their eyewitnesses knew for sure they saw him do it, but when the DNA tests came back it turns out they were completely off target."

"So if they can't actually tell us dogs apart, then if we manage to lose the ID, they lose the dog." I'm finally catching on, here.

"Exactly. And there are always people waiting in line to adopt some nice little doggy. Not so much the same story with cats, but, to be honest, I think we sometimes bring that on ourselves. But with a dog, as long as we can train him to wag his tail and make with the big brown moon eyes, he's in like Flint. And, by the way, this looks like our last stop. Let's find this prison."

South Chicago, 8:30 a.m.

We're slinking along the back fence at Southside Prison, trying to stay low and out of sight of the prison guards. The grass has been left unmowed back here, which helps, plus the guards' eyes are all focused inside the prison, not outside. For some reason they still believe their biggest threats are going to come from the inmates locked away safely in their cells. But we're about to teach them otherwise. Of course, that's assuming old humans can still learn new tricks.

Antonio has a spot picked out on the far corner of the fence where a tree branch fell several years back and gashed a small tear in the perimeter. Too small for most dogs, but if I squeeze in at my shoulders I think I can just make it through.

"You sure we can't just widen this hole big enough so's Killer can slip through?" I ask, eyeing the sharp edges respectfully.

"Believe me, been tried. Been failed. Better pets than you and me have been working at this problem for over a year. Plus there's the question of not wanting to call attention to it. Anything powerful enough to cut through all this metal is almost certainly gonna bring someone over to inspect, and then the jig is up. So this is what we're stuck with. And that still beats the situation we had before that bough broke and this baby did fall."

Not for the first time I tell myself this cat must have some kinda screw loose, 'cause his words make no sense at all. But I save my breath and focus again on the situation at hand. I turn back to him one last time before heading in. "Listen, Antonio, you'd better stay back here." I hook a thumb over my right shoulder. "It's all one big dog party back there, and if you show up unannounced it ain't gonna be pretty. Best we not attract any more attention than necessary."

"Got ya." Antonio runs his eyes quickly over the long line of cages just fifty feet away. "Yeah, I'll keep sentry duty out here, watching the guardhouse and the route back to the fence. You hear a low meow, drop everything and skedaddle back here.

We're way too far into this to risk getting picked up on a stupid criminal trespassing charge at this point."

"Roger that. Well, you got my six, so it's time to get a move on." I gotta say I kinda like the old military lingo. Not something you get to use every day. "Okay, big guy. I'll be back in a flash." The killing field in front of me is clear, and there's no Gestapo to be seen anywhere. I let out a couple of quick, low arfs. Nothing to draw attention, but I'm hoping Killer will pick up on my call and spread the word that I'm to be trusted among his prison mates. Keep the usual insulting perp walk chatter to a minimum, so hopefully I can get in and out with no one being the wiser.

Each cell has a private opening to let the dogs in the cell block get in some quality outside time, and I suspect that breakfast rations have just been served up, since every dog is apparently inside. No Killer anywhere to be seen. I pick out a random cell near the middle of the run and squeeze up close to the fence, letting out a muffled 'ruff' to draw some attention from the guy inside. An Irish Retriever pokes his head out briefly, looking around for the source of the sound, and spots me immediately.

"Top o' th' mornin' to ya!" he calls out. "By me sainted mother, what you be doing out there on walkies without a guard?"

"Shhhh," I whisper. "I'm trying to make contact with one of the inmates, a friend of mine. A pit bull named Killer. You know him?"

"No," she — I look again — he answers. "But the pit balls all be quartered in their oown section, off oon the left. The humans be thinking they be a menace to everyone, so's…"

"Right. I get it. Just more of the usual for those guys. Racial profiling, toss the innocent in with the guilty. No problem, I'll go look for him over there." I try to catch a peek through the hole at the other side, the inside of the cell block runs. "Any guards hanging around right now?"

"No, after breakfast they all headed back to the gard' house," Red tells me, checking once more around him, just to be sure. "But I'll send a wee message down the line, lettin' him know you're comin'."

"That would be swell. Thanks, buddy." I give him a good fast wag of my tail and head off left along the fence line. I can hear small ruffs and growls coming from my right as notice of my mission is relayed ahead.

The pit bull section is completely separated from the rest of the dogs, with signs along the walkway leading to their cages, warning the humans of danger. Signs with dogs showing their full God-given array of pearly whites. A look that to us dogs could mean just about anything, but the humans of course always seem to expect the worst of folks.

I spot Killer almost immediately, slunk down on the floor of his cell with a full bowl of kibble lying in front of him, untouched. As I dart from the safety of the main runs and across the empty and exposed field to the pit bull cages beyond, I let out a few low arfs to wake him up, but Killer doesn't bat an ear.

The whole area is thankfully completely free of humans, and word has apparently reached the Pits ahead of me, courtesy of Red. The Pits are all up and wagging, all except one frighteningly large almost midnight black dog at the end of the line, who's sending a message with his pearly whites — or in his case, yellows — that can only be interpreted one way. The truth is, there are some dogs running around this world who really do need to be locked up. It's a dangerous world out there, but it's a lot less dangerous with dogs like Midnight safely locked behind bars.

"Hey, Yorkie. Over here!" A gray and tan pit bull right next to Killer's cell is motioning me over. I decide to ignore the slur. Pit bulls are notoriously unreliable, depending upon how they've been treated growing up. Very high incidence of PTSD with those dogs, probably has something to do with how they're all so sensitive. Always got their hearts on their sleeves. Or on their forelegs, to be exact. But Gray seems friendly enough, and his tail is wagging canine Morse code almost faster than I can decode it.

"You the little sidekick Killer's always going on about?" Gray asks.

"Guess so," I answer, ignoring the implied insult. That's twice now with this dog, pretty much my limit. I glance back at Killer, but he hasn't moved. "How long's he been like that?"

"Pretty much since he came in," Gray answers, his tail now silent. "I hear things don't look too good for him."

I touch muzzles with him briefly, letting him know I appreciate his caring for my friend. "Well, hopefully we can turn that around for him before it's… too late, you know."

"Yeah. We see a lot o' guys wind up taking the walk down the Green Aisle, and then we never see 'em again. What's he in for, if you don' mind me askin'?"

"He got set up by the CC's for killing his girlfriend, a Frenchie. Good looking girl, if you like the type. Anyway, we found the real killer, but there's no way to get the humans to pay attention to the evidence in time. So we're trying to work up a plan to spring him out."

"A French bulldog, you say?" Gray thinks about this a second, rubbing his muzzle. "Hmmm. Nice personalities and all, but I can't quite get myself to imagine one of those I'd call good lookin'. Flat face and all, ever one of 'ems look like they got caught chasin' a car when it slammed on its brakes. Not to mention their bodies, which aren't exactly what you'd call bikini friendly…"

"No, no, not French bulldog," I correct him. "French poodle. Standard size."

"Oooh, I get ya. A poodle. Makes sense. But," he hesitates and looks over toward the main cell blocks. "Better you not let any of the bulldogs over there find out you called a poodle a Frenchie. They get pretty sensitive about that kind of thing."

"Good to know." I make a note to check into this. I've never actually met a French bulldog before, so maybe I've been using the wrong term for poodles all along. Maybe Mom was right, maybe I'd be better off just getting rid of the slang altogether. Beats looking like a fool to all the guys on the street, that's for sure. I drop the subject and point back to Killer. "Any luck getting his attention?"

"Nah, he doesn't even look up when they bring the dinner bowls. Just lays there mopin' all day, cryin' into his own slobber. Think he's scared of what's comin'?"

"Killer ain't scared of nuthin' or nobody," I answer. "But he just saw his girlfriend cut down in cold blood, right before his eyes. Gotta have some impact on pretty much anyone, you know? Gimme a second…"

I move over in front of Killer's cell, getting as close as I possibly can to him. "Hey! Killer. Buddy," I whisper, keeping one eye trained on the guardhouse door behind me. "It's Moose. I've come to help you, buddy."

Slowly I see one ear start to twitch. I check his paws to see if he's dreaming, but they're completely quiet. "Buddy. Killer. Come on, wake up."

After what seems like a lifetime of eternities, his left eye pops open. Then his right. At first I think he might be blind, that the coppers did something to him in the back of the wagon on his way to Southside, but then he seems to focus, and suddenly his head pops up, too.

"Moose! What are you doing here?"

"Came to get you outta here, buddy. Got some people working on a prison break. But I need your help."

He draws himself up on all four and slowly staggers over to where I'm sitting. It's obvious that his joints must be stiff from lying in one position for so long.

"Man, you can't be seen around here," he tells me, poking his muzzle through the fence for a quick nose bump. "They catch you here, that's the second time for you. Third time gets you life."

"Willing to risk it," I assure him, but I check the guardhouse again, just to be safe. "They treating you okay around here?"

"Can't complain, really." Killer looks back at his bowl, still full of kibble. "Food seems okay, but I haven't had much of an appetite." He hangs his head low, his eyes now shut tight. "Alls I can think about is

Penny, you know. Alls I can think about is her lyin' there, an' nothin' I could do to help…"

I try to think of what to say here, and I'm coming up empty. Never had to console a victim before. Can't say I ever want to try it again, either. Finally I decide that focusing on the future is gonna work out a whole lot better than dwelling on the past. Plenty of time to mourn Penny later on, when Killer's free of this joint.

"Look, Killer, I don't have much time before this whole place is stinking with humans, literally, so I gotta be quick." I point to the ground beneath the concrete slab he's standing on. "I got a source tells me there's a giant tunnel just underneath this place." I make a decision on the spot to keep mum about it being a sewer and all. Some details just don't need to be shared. By the time he finds out, it'll all seem like the smell of freedom to him, anyway. "The thing is, we gotta blast a hole in the ground to get to ya, to open a direct escape route to down below. And the blast is gonna come from underneath, inside the tunnel. So here's the problem..." I quickly sketch out the plan. After dinner that night, when the humans have finished their last rounds of the cell blocks and have gone inside for the night, Killer is gonna grab his food bowl in his jaws and beat it hard against the ground for ten to fifteen minutes. That will let the demolition team down below set the explosives in just the right spot. When he's finished, Killer will then retreat through his hole to the outside, huddling in the far corner of his outside run, clear of the blast.

"When you hear the explosion, come back through the doggie hole to the inside of the cell. We should have opened a crater in the ground big enough for you to drop through. I'll have an extraction team down there waiting for you. And Killer," I pause to make sure he's paying attention. "Time is of the essence. Once that explosion goes off, the humans will be swarming all over this place like flies on a pile of horse hockey. You gotta hit that hole at full speed. Any questions?"

He's been looking away the whole time I've been wuffing. Finally he turns and looks me in the eye. His are completely bloodshot. “How’s Penny?” he asks.

Suddenly I realize he doesn’t know, he thinks she may still be alive. And I also realize that this isn’t at all the right time to deal with that particular issue. As Ted Kennedy once said, we’ll cross that bridge when we come to it. Right now I’ve got a prison break to run.

“Killer, we’ll talk about all that later tonight. When you’re on the other side of these walls. Just remember, bang your bowl when the coast is clear, then get back out of the way. And spread the word to your buddies, too. No sense in their getting caught up in the collateral damage.” I realize I’ve been spending so much time with Antonio, I’m actually starting to sound like him. One scary thought. But now I see the door knob on the guardhouse start to turn, so it’s time to make my own escape for now.

“Okay, buddy. Gotta go. Just a few more hours and we’ll be lapping adult beverages out of the old toilet bowl together. Just like old times.”

Killer has seen the movement from the guardhouse, too, and motions toward the far fence with his muzzle. "Thanks, little buddy! Now get going! Run, Moose, run!"

And I do, just as fast as my short but well-muscled little legs will carry me. I make it to the fence line and through unseen, then look back. Killer is standing in his cell, smiling at me and waving. Maybe smiling for the last time, after what I'll have to tell him about Penny later tonight.

The Miracle Mile, 11:00 a.m.

Word on the street is, anything you need in Chicago, Tommy Tuxedo can get it. For a price. I'm not completely sure how I'm gonna come up with the big bucks to pay him, but at this point I don't have a lot of choice. It's not like you can just waltz into a seven 'leven and pick up a stick or two of dynamite right off the shelf. There's procedures to be followed for these kinds of things. It's all about supply and demand, and creating artificial scarcity. Driving the price of something you need to get your hands on right away sky high. Antonio doesn't seem worried, though.

"The thing is, you don't really have any options, here," he explains. "You could wait a few days, maybe the price will drop a little, save ya a few bucks, you know? But by then you won't be needing the nitro. So, the price is the price, and the only thing we get to negotiate is the interest on the note."

"Interest? Note? What note?" I ask. Antonio seems to have forgotten to share this one interesting little detail with me.

Antonio looks my way and I can swear I catch him rolling his eyes for a second. "Well, since you don't have any, what we might call *liquid* capital, or really, any kind of capital at all, then your only option here is to take out an unsecured loan."

"I'm gonna borrow money from a loan shark?" I ask, incredulous that he would even suggest the idea.

"Not exactly a shark," Antonio answers, his attention everywhere but my direction. "More what I'd call an orca. A killer whale. Runs a little action from over at the Shedd Aquarium."

"But if I take out a loan, and don't make my payments, won't he take out my knees?" I protest, starting to gather some looks from the other dogs around us, all out on walkies with their mistresses and masters.

"Yeah, well, I wouldn't worry about your knees," he explains, suddenly darting between two cars that are stopped at a light. "Orcas got no use for knees. Too bony, no nutrition. No, those orcas, they tend to swallow you whole."

Once again I'm thanking the Lord for having missed a few meals, as my stomach flips over once or twice and my legs go a little weak on me. I stumble a second but manage to somehow stay upright, and follow him between the cars.

"But Antonio, say I go along with this — and to be fair I don't see that I have much choice right now — how will we know how much to borrow before we get a chance to talk to the Tuxedo?"

"We won't," he answers, disappearing into a small crack in the wall of what appears to be a fancy jewelry store of some kind. I follow him through, and immediately just barely miss bumping into his back. Antonio has stopped in an empty hallway and appears to be looking around for something.

"Been a while since I was here — should be right about..." A small door opens in the wall off to our left, and Antonio shoots me a beckoning look and saunters inside.

The office is furnished ultramodern, all glass and chrome and black and white, with small splashes of bright colors here and there, startling in their own stark way. There's a desk in front of us, looks like it's pure cut crystal, and behind it sits Tommy Tuxedo himself.

Even I have heard of this particular cat. He's a legend, kind of like Fat Tony. Tommy's got a computer screen set up to his left and is using a mouse to scroll through its contents. Not a real mouse — the computer kind, you know. A real mouse would be next to useless.

Tommy is a classic Tuxedo, mostly ink black with a snow white chest and white paws. His fur has the kind of silken sheen you only get from being exceptionally well fed, but he's showing no evidence of being fat or lazy. He's thin, but it's clear that there's quite a bit of quiet power lurking behind that fur. And even more power lurking behind those emerald eyes.

After a long while he finally seems to notice us and looks up, turning the monitor slightly to keep us from seeing what he's been pouring over. Which makes me even more curious to find out what it is that has had him so absorbed. As any of my friends will tell ya, sometimes I can be every bit as curious as a house cat. But that kind of curiosity has a habit of getting you killed, and I've had way too much of that kind of action over the last day or so for my own comfort. I decide it's wisest to let the Tuxedo keep his own secrets for the time being.

Antonio jumps up into a hard plastic chair, all white curves with bright chrome trappings. I study the matching chair to its left and decide the floor is a much softer option. My plan is to let Antonio do all the talking, anyway. I just hope all this doesn't end up with me in the boca of an orca, as our new friend Fisheye would say.

Tommy Tuxedo clears his throat — or maybe it's just a hairball he's fussing with — and nods toward Antonio. "What can I do you for, gentlemen?"

"Yeah, look, Tommy," Antonio begins, wiggling around in the chair like he's still trying to find some way to get comfortable. It occurs to me that the two chairs facing the crystal desk had probably been designed for just that purpose, to put Tommy's guests at a maximum state of unease. I'm liking my decision to stick with the floor even better at this point.

Finally Antonio seems to have found a soft spot, or at least a less hard spot, and he settles in, leaning over slightly and resting his left paw on the desk. "We got ourselves a kinda... *situation*, and we'd like you to help us out a bit."

"Situation, eh? I like the sound of that." Tommy looks like he's already counting the profits on this deal, the toes on his right front paw rubbing against themselves slightly in anticipation.

Antonio hasn't missed the paw movement, either. "Okay, the deal is, you and I go back a long ways, *capisce*? And I've always liked the way you operate. Fair and square, value given for value received."

Tommy leans back in his white leather Scandinavian desk chair, his head tilting a bit to the right as he studies my partner. Kind of like he's studying a bowl of tuna, wondering where to take the first bite. "The way any good business deal should be, my friend. Equally beneficial to both sides, eh? Or equally painful, depending upon how it all plays out in the end. So, which is it, Fat Tony? Beneficial? Or painful?"

"Oh, nothing all that complicated, Tommy," Antonio answers quickly. Maybe too quickly. I can count my life savings trickling away as they speak. "It's all pretty straightforward, actually," he continues. "We just need to get our hands on a certain — object, that we can't easily pick up at the corner market."

"Object, eh?" Tommy looks intrigued now, and reaches down to pick up a glass of some clear liquid. Water, maybe. Or maybe not. "What kind of object are we talking about?"

Antonio hesitates a half second, then blurts it out in a low mumble. "A bomb."

The Tuxedo's face explodes and the clear liquid spurts across the desk, some of it splashing all the way over to me. I sniff at my fur. A martini, it seems. Dirty, with just a hint of something spicy. Real classy.

"That's all you want?" Tommy's mouth is hanging open as he talks, his paws waving wildly in the air. "That's all you want? A *bomb*? Well, why didn't you say so before? I think I may just have one sitting here in my desk drawer..."

I lick at my fur, cleaning the martini off it. Not so much because I like the taste, which I don't — it tastes a little like the way gasoline smells — but I need to have something to do while Antonio deals with the Tuxedo.

"Heh heh, Tommy, *mi vecchio amico*." Antonio is smiling, but a wary look is guarding his eyes. "You know I wouldn't ask if it wasn't important—"

"Important? What you're asking for would net me the rest of my life in Guantanamo if I ever got caught with it. Or worse!" Tommy is up and stalking back and forth in front of his desk, wringing his paws. "Just *talking* about having a bomb is a federal crime these days. You know I don't deal in anything like that."

Antonio is watching the Tuxedo pace back and forth, like watching a tennis game from the center seats. "Yeah, well then I was hopin' maybe you might know someone who does. You see, my *compagno* here is in a real tight place, and I was thinking maybe you could see your way clear to helping him out a bit."

"Yeah? And why is that?" Tommy asks, his upper lip lifted in an obvious sneer.

"Because he's got a friend stuck in the same situation a certain young kitty was in, back when we just were bambini working the docks. Back when I put *my* fur on the line to help out a certain friend in need."

A long look passes between them. Finally, Tommy seems to melt, and I can see my friend finally starting to relax beside me.

"Fine, fine. I'll see what I can do." Tommy sits back down and grabs the keyboard to his computer. "The thing is, I don't have a line on anything like that. Nor do I know anyone that does. The good old days when the Mob could firebomb someone at will or take them down in a hail of bullets, those days are history. Homeland Security and the Bureau got their fingers in too many pies these days to risk playing around in the pie business. But I do have some ideas that might work."

He starts tapping furiously on the keyboard with his front claws. "I'm thinking there's no way we can go professional without winding up in the anti terror net. But that doesn't mean we can't figure out how to cook something up at home." He gets busy again on the keyboard, pausing every now and then to stare at the screen, then shakes his head sharply and moves on.

"Let's see here… there's the old baking soda vinegar bomb. Nah, not powerful enough. And way too messy, believe me. Been there, done that. Hmmm. Says here we could build ourselves a meth lab, then blow it up… rednecks do it all the time. Unintentionally, of course. And here's a list of ingredients… yeah, got that, got that, got that…" He points to the screen. “Well, we’ve got everything we need but the Sudafed. But that stuff’s tightly controlled, so one of you will have to somehow convince a pharmacist—”

“Not going to happen,” Antonio growls.

“Yeah, right, probably a bad idea all around.” Tommy leans closer to the screen, still slowly scrolling down the page. “Won’t work… too hard… no, kinda need thumbs for that…” Suddenly he shoots straight up in his chair. “Aha! Here it is! Really simple ingredients, easy to make, don’t need any money — that one is a real game changer, once you think about it — and it should make for a blast that’s fairly easily controlled but still strong enough to get the job done.”

“What is it? What did you find, Tommy?” I ask, unable to keep myself from hopping up and down.

“The old standby, you know,” Tommy answers, his eyes wide with excitement. “I kinda feel ashamed I didn’t think of it before.” Tommy is rubbing the side of his head, in the process flipping his left ear back and forth. It's kinda distracting. "All told, it's one of the easiest bombs you can make without a lab. And all you need is a little run-of-the-mill gasoline and… a bucket load of chicken poop!"

Fat Tony's Office, 12:45 p.m.

We all decided to meet back up at Antonio's office. It's midday on Sunday, and the place is deserted. Important if you've got a room full of assorted cats, dogs and whatever and you want to keep the whole thing completely off the human radar grid.

Antonio has found a cardboard box he's propped up on a chair and is standing on the box scribbling assignments on a whiteboard, using a plain black marker. I sneak a quick look to be sure, and I don't have the nerve to let him know it's a permanent marker. After all, the damage has already been done by this point. The handwriting's on the wall, you could say.

We've managed to pull together a pretty good crew for the prison break. Every animal in the room has at one point or another either been in prison themselves, or has someone they know and love who was. So springing Killer out of the hoosegow is personal to all of us.

Bella isn't quite sold on the project, however. She still has doubts, and isn't at all hesitant to express them. Although she does seem to have mellowed a tiny bit from earlier. Not that I don't still hear that voice ringing in my ears. And every time it does I start to salivate for some reason.

She's got me pinned, and is letting me have it one more time. "Look Moose, I know you have faith in your buddy, but I also know what I saw with my own eyes. Killer standing over Penny's body, with blood dripping off his lips. Are you trying to tell me I should trust your story more than my own eyes?"

Antonio looks like he's about to cut in, but I hold up a paw to stop him. This is my argument. And Killer and Bella are both my friends.

"Bella, I know what you think you saw. But appearances can be deceiving. I mean, remember that Sheltie you were so sweet on a while back? Didn't see *that* one coming, did you?" Bella blushes bright red, and I hate doing this to her, but I have no choice. Plus I'm rapidly running out of time. "And remember that time you could have sworn that visiting

Dalmation ate your kibble, told every dog in the neighborhood she did it, then it turned out to be a thieving raccoon that had just moved into the area?" Bella is starting to bob her head in agreement, so I move in quickly for the close. "And Bella, look, I swear to you, I *heard* it loud and clear with my own two ears, that Crimson Canine admitting that it was his friend what killed Penny. Antonio heard it, too, plain as day."

"And why would the CC's do that?" Bella argued, almost but not yet completely convinced.

I glance around at the crowd, about ready to spill the whole story. Then I remember Killer, still holding out hope that Penny had survived. That was love talking, pure unadulterated love. The kind of love hardly any of us ever get to see in our entire lives. If I spill the beans here, there's no way I can keep the whole sordid tale from making its way back to Killer some day. A story that would break his heart all over again.

I guess that's why they call us private eyes, you know? It's our job to pry into people's deepest, darkest secrets, to get answers to questions most people would rather keep buried deep in their past. But sometimes those answers need to *stay* buried, at least to people who don't need to know. Sometimes what we find out is for our eyes only, and keeping those discoveries secret is every bit as important to the job as what we wind up telling. For Killer, the truth about Penny's struggles with addiction, the fact that she agreed for a time to help the CC's hang that yoke on other innocent souls just to feed her own cravings for the crack, that was a truth that could no longer help anyone.

"Bella, you just have to take my word on it. And Antonio's. And — Fisheye over there." Fisheye nods his head solemnly. "Maybe someday I can sit down with you and explain it all. But right now, for Killer's sake — for *Penny's* sake, God rest her soul — we just need our memories of her to stay clear of this whole ugly mess. Even in death she deserves at least that, don't you think?"

Bella chews on that for a second, then finally nods her agreement.

"Okay," I continue, relieved that we've finally managed to get all of that behind us. "So the next step is to figure out who's gonna do what. And Antonio is the mastermind for all of that, so I'll turn it all over to him."

Antonio straightens up on the cardboard box. He's put the cap back on the permanent marker, and is using it now as a pointer. "Okay, team, this is all pretty simple. There are three major elements to this whole operation, and everyone here is going to have a critical role in pulling it off successfully. I can't emphasize enough that one little slip up on anyone's part can bring the whole thing crashing down to a screeching halt. Loose slips sink ships, *capisce*?"

I'm standing behind the whole group now, watching, and everyone in the room appears to be nodding, excited to be a part of Killer's rescue. Antonio sees it too, and continues. "All right. Let's do it, then." He points to the first item on the list behind him. "The first assignment. Making the bomb. Now that actually breaks down into several smaller assignments, which is true of the entire assault plan.

Assignment number one is to collect the gasoline. I can't think of anyone better suited to that than Fabio, our Saint Bernard, here. Got your little jug ready, *mi piccolo ragazzo*?"

Fabio points to the keg hanging from his neck with one paw and smiles a wide kibble-eating grin. "Ready, sir!"

"Good." Antonio shifts to look behind him. "Now, Tommy Tuxedo has volunteered to actually cook the bomb, using a recipe he pulled down off the Internet. I don't have to tell anyone that Tommy has taken on what is likely the most dangerous assignment. One little booboo and *blam*, it's all over. So if any of us had hats, Tommy, we'd take them off for you right now to show you our thanks."

Tommy holds up his paws, shrugging it all off, but I can tell he's basking in all of the attention right now.

When everything quiets back down, Antonio points to the third item on the bomb making list. "Third, we need someone to go collect the chicken poop. This is the source of the phosphates and nitrogen that power the bomb, and it's every bit as important, if not more important, than the gasoline. And for that key assignment, we need someone who has shown her courage and bravery every step of the way. A dog that is loyal and fearless. A dog that is not afraid to get down and dirty when duty calls. And I can't think of a better soldier to call on for this job than our own stouthearted little Corgi, Bella. Bella, stand up and let us salute you, girl!"

Bella looks completely surprised by all this. "But I didn't — I mean, I can't be — I mean, chicken poop?" But her protests are being drowned out by the applause from all of us in the room, applause I made sure to take the lead on from the outset, and she quickly realizes that there's no way she can turn the assignment down without looking totally ungrateful in front of all her neighbors and friends. She's stuck, and now she'll just have to buck up and carry through on the assignment. I feel kinda sorry for her, though. She really got completely hoodwinked into accepting this dirty, dirty job. When it's all over and Killer is walking free, I know I'll have to find some way to make it up to her.

In the meantime, Antonio has quickly gone around the room and finished off his task list. Everyone has a key role to play in the breakout. Now we all just have to execute. And do it quickly, before Killer gets executed himself.

Prison Break HQ, 4:15 p.m.

Ike has managed to carve out some space for us back in the Bush to assemble the bomb and coordinate the plan of attack. Fisheye agreed to help Fabio with hunting down the gasoline, and after several trips back and forth, siphoning gas from lawn mowers stashed in outdoor shacks and from one or two unsuspecting mopeds, they finally have enough collected to build the bomb.

Antonio is starting to get nervous about Bella, though. She's been gone for several hours, targeting a short list of urban chicken coops we've scouted out, but nobody has heard from nor seen her since the time the meeting broke up just after lunch. I'm almost ready to send out a search party for her when all of a sudden I hear a ruckus coming from the vicinity of the front door.

I rush over there as fast as my little legs can take me, just in time to see Bella wander through the door. Her plus-sized body is covered in chicken poop and feathers, and I'm just about to break out in laughter when I notice the tears pouring like a waterfall from her eyes.

"Guys, guys, give her room!" I holler out, trying to make sure everyone else treats her with the respect she deserves. After all, she didn't actually volunteer for this awful assignment, but instead got roped into it, kicking and screaming, and now I'm feeling the greatest shame of my entire life for having been a part of that.

I race up to her and hug her, heartily, not giving a single thought to what I'm now getting all over my own fur. "Bella! Thank God! We were so worried…"

"I — I'm okay—" she says in a voice that is totally unconvincing. "But — Moose — I — I did it."

She points behind her toward the doorway, where there's a large bucket filled to the brim with some white chalky substance — and not just a few stray feathers — sitting off all by itself, with the cats and dogs standing nearby obviously struggling to maintain a safe distance away from it.

"I knew you could do it, Bella," I whisper to her as I nuzzle her — really filthy — ear a little. "I knew you were the one we could count on, the only one who could get it done." I pull back slightly and the crowd starts to part like Noah and the Red Sea. Did I get that right? Anyway, everyone seems happy to give us some space, so I grab her paw and start to lead her through it. "Now let's get you cleaned up and get some warm wet food down you. You'll feel much better when we're all done."

"Th-thank you, Moose," is all she can say.

I hear a voice behind us yelling "Hazmat team on the double! Code S!" But right now all I'm thinking about is sweet Bella, who sacrificed so much to save a dog she isn't even sure should be saved. And how many people would ever do that, especially humans? She's my hero, I decide. Bella's my true American hero.

Prison Break HQ, 5:45 p.m.

"So, Tommy, what's the status on the bomb?" Antonio asks. We're all gathered around, walking through the last details on Operation Alice. As in Wonderland. As in down the rabbit hole. We gotta be a little indirect in naming these things, just in case we have a security leak and word gets out to the enemy.

Tommy Tuxedo is consulting his notes. "Well, FT, thanks to all the hard work Bella and Fabio put in, we wound up at almost 150% of target. And, by the way, can I ask everyone to give Bella another well-deserved round of applause?" Everyone immediately jumps to their feet, and the place is ringing with clapping and an occasional loud 'hoozah!' Bella has recovered somewhat from her ordeal, and is sitting off in one corner, blushing. I look over and try to give her a thumbs up sign, but of course I fail. No thumbs, you know. Tommy's still talking. "I have to tell ya, Bella, never thought I'd ever say this to a dog, but today you made me proud to say you're my friend."

That sets off another sharp round of applause, and I take the opportunity to cut through the crowd and slide in next to Bella, putting an arm gently around her. She looks up at me and gives me a smile that sends a shiver down my muzzle and all the way to the tip of my stubby tail.

Antonio has moved on to other assignments, and as the various teams check in, the operation appears to be a go. I give Bella a quick lick on the ear, then turn to find my partners for the above ground assault team. Before I leave, though, she snags my collar and pulls me back.

"Moose, thank you. Thank you for everything."

I can't help it. I'm grinning from ear to ear right now, and my tail is starting to vibrate like a Samsung washing machine. "No, Bella, thank you. Tommy was right — if we succeed today, if Killer gets free, it's all because of you. You're a true blue friend."

“No, Moose, that honor belongs to you. Look at everything you’ve done, all the risks you’ve taken. Almost getting yourself killed. I — I was really hard on you back then. Before. Back in our yards. But the thing is, you were just being loyal to your friend, standing up for him when no one else would. And Moose, when all of this is over, when we’re all back in the neighborhood safe and sound, I’m going to find some way to show you how much that means to me. I’m a Corgi, after all, and if you can say anything at all about a Corgi, it’s that she’s loyal. But the truth is, I’ve never met a dog, Corgi or otherwise, who’s even half as loyal as you.”

I don’t really know what to say, and to be honest my voice box seems to have locked up somehow, so I just give her a quick muzzle and turn to go before she can see that there’s something terribly wrong with my eyes as well.

Rendezvous Point, 7:00 p.m.

We're all down on one knee, watching and listening, while Antonio is parading back and forth in front of us, slapping a long pointer against his leg as he walks. "Moose, I need you and Jacques to cover the topside recon, and be prepared once the bomb goes off to make sure Killer hits the hole fast and furious. Tommy and my sewer rat connection, Pops, will be setting the bomb and handling the detonation. The rest of us will be standing by just outside the range of the explosion for extraction and recovery. Any questions? This is your last chance people. Any questions at all before we break off for our respective assignments?"

Everyone is shaking their heads no. We've been training for this moment all afternoon. No, really, in many ways we've been training for this moment all our lives, and now it all comes down to this. Operation Alice is a go. Now we just have to execute like all our lives depend upon it. And, for Killer at least, it does.

I left Bella sitting at a table back at HQ. Her mission assignment was over, and it just didn't seem fair to ask her to put any more on the line than she already had. She gave me the usual guff about promising to stay safe and come back to her in one piece, and I gave her a quick scuff between her ears with my paw, then trotted out as quickly as I could, not daring to look back.

Tommy and Pops, Antonio's Papillon sewer expert, are waiting at the entrance to the tunnel. It looks like nothing more than a spot where the sewer had collapsed a bit, with a large bush blocking the entrance from plain sight. We slip down easily into the hole, and I have to rest for a moment to let my eyes adjust to the darkness. I try a few test sniffs, but overall it doesn't smell all that bad, mostly dank and moldy, nothing I can't deal with.

Pops is taking the lead, with Tommy following close behind. I rush to catch up with them, careful not to cut my paws on the broken glass and other assorted debris littering the floor of the tunnel. Other than the trash, the place looks more like a grand ballroom than a sewer, with vaulted ceilings fading into the shadows at least twenty to thirty feet above my head and drifting off a similar distance to either side of us. Ancient shelves, crumbling and lined with cobwebs, cover almost every wall, and in front of them are what looks like wooden breakfast counters, with old wooden stools drawn up tight underneath. Every now and then I come upon a pile of tables, two to three feet wide, stacked up one on top of the other and stretching upwards as far as I can see. Alongside them are chairs, lots of old chairs. And all of this is covered with a thick coating of must and mold. Pumping my little legs to stay up with Pops and Tommy, it's all I can do to keep from accidentally brushing up against one of those towers of tables and sending the whole mess crashing down on me.

As we get deeper into the tunnel the light gets even dimmer. Finally we bend to the right into a side branch that slopes up slightly from the main tunnel, almost pitch black now and still almost twenty feet across.

"This should be about it," Pops calls out, his wheezy voice echoing all through the tunnels. "This line runs right under the prison. Now we just gotta wait for the signal from your guy upstairs."

This is the first time I've had a chance to get a good look at Pops, and as my eyes adjust to the faint light drifting in from the main tunnel I stop for a second to check him out. Antonio tells me that "Papillon" means butterfly, and I guess that's because Papillon dogs like Pops are a little bit flitty, if you know what I mean. He has huge ears that sprout from the top of his head like giant wings, which is why Antonio picked him for this assignment — with those ears he can pick up even the slightest sound, and hopefully he'll be able to hear Killer banging his food bowl against his cell floor through God knows how many layers of dirt and concrete that lie above us.

"Now we wait," Pops tells us, coughing slightly at the effort. I start to sit while we're waiting, then luckily glance down. Something's creeping along the floor that I can't quite make out, but I think I can see some green and red and a lot of legs, so I decide to move a little more to the right and stay standing.

After a while I think I can pick up the faintest sound of something drumming out a bad rhythm from up above. Tommy hears it, too, and leans in toward Pops. "Is that our guy?" he asks in a low voice, which still manages to echo down the empty tunnel.

"Eh?" Pops answers. He fiddles with something in his left ear. "What cha say, boy?" he asks.

"I SAID, IS THAT OUR SIGNAL?" Tommy repeats, his booming voice sounding like a cannon going off all around us. He's got a claw out pointing upward toward the ceiling.

"Eh? Does what tickle?" Pops answers, then finally notices Tommy's upraised paw. "Oh. Yeah. Already on it, sonny. No need to shout." He starts to move about the tunnel, training his ears toward the sound coming from above and muttering something about whippersnappers. His face all is scrunched up, turning an already impressive network of creases and wrinkles into something that now better resembles the Grand Canyon. It's not a good look, but, in some way that I can't really put a paw on, it works for him.

Finally he stops and points to a location almost directly above his head. "There's yer target, boys. Let 'er blow!"

"Are you sure?" Tommy asks, double checking. When Pops doesn't answer, he leans in closer. "I SAID, ARE YOU SURE?" I don't know about him, but I could have sworn the banging sound was coming from somewhere further off down the tunnel.

"What? You doubtin' me, son? I say, you Johnny-wet-behind-the-ears sayin' I can't do my job?" Pops has his chest all puffed out, and is walking around in circles chasing his tail and barking to himself. "Why, I'll have you know I was the top dog in sonar school, back in the day. Taught the class, in fact. Could spot a squirrel from two miles away. Now these jump-up whelps be questionin' my hearin'!

Have half a mind to turn them all over my knee, give 'em something real to yelp about!"

I try to shut him out and turn back to see what Tommy is doing. He has the bomb bucket in his left paw and is examining a rickety pile of tables stacked up directly under the explosion target.

"Hey, Tommy, we gotta do something to shore this thing up," I warn him, stepping back what I think is a safe distance away. "Just one touch and it's all gonna come down on us like an avalanche. Maybe there's a ladder somewhere around here we can use."

I stop for a second to look around the tunnel for anything even remotely resembling a ladder, and when I turn back, Tommy's completely disappeared. You know, I've been worrying the whole time we've been here whether or not this floor is safe — worrying is really one of my best qualities — and now it looks like I was right all along!

I strain my eyes to try and see though the dust-filled gloom, trying to find the place where he must've fallen in, but I'm more of an ear and nose guy, and I can't see a thing other than a couple of those green and red buggers darting back and forth.

"Pops! Tommy's been eaten alive!" I yell out, bringing in reinforcements.

"What in the Sam Hill are you talking about?" comes a voice from way above my head. I look straight up, and sitting at the very top of the tower of half-rotten tables is none other than Tommy, still waving the bomb in his left paw while using his right to probe for cracks in the ceiling above him. The tower is swaying slightly back and forth like a tree in a light breeze, but Tommy doesn't seem to notice. Every time it moves in one direction, he does a little wiggle with his hips and the whole stack comes right back to center.

"How in the world did you get all the way up there?" I call up to him, still careful not to get too close.

"What do you mean?" Tommy calls back. "I'm a cat!"

He's got me there. I can barely make it up on the couch these days without a little assistance, and you can forget the master's bed. Gotta get an emergency airlift to boost me into place every night and then back down every morning. But for sure I'm not gonna admit that to this cat.

"Do you need some help up there?" I offer meekly, holding a paw up over my eyes to help me see. Tommy, being mostly black, keeps coming and going in my vision, but sometimes he turns my way and I can just barely make out the patch of white fur on his chest.

"Nope, I got it, Moose," he answers back. "But don't you have to see a jail about a dog right about now?"

"Oh, yeah, you're right. Sorry!" I turn around slowly to get my bearings in the dark. Straight back down the side tunnel, then a sharp left and straight again until I'm out. As I head that way I can still hear Pops rambling on behind me.

"I'm just glad the little Lady didn't live long enough to see what I have to put up with these days. Why, I've got a boil on my butt gots more sense than these young 'uns ever will have. Got no respect for their elders, that's what the problem is. And it's their parent's fault, for sure. Puppies grow up, parents just give 'em everything they want, don't have to work for a thing. Why, back in my day, you wanted a chew stick, you had to *earn* it. And none of those namby pamby rawhide sticks, neither. The real thing! Oak, maple, whatever you could find out in the yard. Chew that thing down to a nub, we did..."

Outside Southside Prison, 8:20 p.m.

I make it back to the hole in the fence behind Southside Prison in record time, and this time I'm not going in alone. Antonio is waiting for me, along with Jacques, a French Chihuahua. Yeah, I know, never heard of that before, either, but then these days it seems like there's a lot I don't know. I guess I've been pretty sheltered over the years, to tell you the truth.

Antonio is sketching the plan out in the dirt. "So, Moose, you head straight to Killer's cell, make sure he's in position for the blast. Jacques and I are taking up forward positions to keep a lookout for first responders. But if you move fast like you should after Killer is down in the tunnel and safe, you'll be well out of the area long before they get even the first inkling that something has happened. The go signal for the detonation is three sharp barks. Once Killer is down the hole, give us two sharp barks, then head back this way and out the hole. Jacques and I will be right behind you."

"Shouldn't we leave someone back here to cover our retreat?" I ask, pointing out the open and exposed field we'll have to race across to make it out of the prison ourselves.

Antonio looks confused. "Well, of course. That's why we have Max, here."

"Glad I could help," comes a voice from out of nowhere, and I leap almost an inch or two straight up into the air. Which, by the way, is a personal best for me in the standing high jump.

Suddenly I see him, crouched down in the weeds not three feet from us. Max, my old Great Pyrenees friend from the city. "My God, Max! I almost wet myself!" I've got a paw pressed close against my thumping heart, and I can see now that Max is grinning from ear to ear. That little hiding and leaping out at the last minute thing is his favorite trick, and I must admit he's pretty darn good at it.

“Okay, small talk later, team,” Antonio orders us curtly. “Time right now to get into position. Moose, you go first.”

I wriggle quickly through the hole and strut my way straight across the walkies field to Killer’s cage. I glance back for a second and see that Antonio and Jacques are already through and headed for the front of the prison, where they can keep an eye out for cops or any other unwanted intruders.

Killer is waiting for me at the front of his cage. His eyes are bright and he’s panting slightly with excitement. I notice that his food bowl’s now empty, a good sign, because he’ll need all the strength he can gather in order for us to pull this caper off. I motion for him to meet me in the outside area, where I pick out the corner that’s furthest away from the blast target and lean in as far as I can to give him his final instructions.

“Okay, Killer. The signal for the blast will be three sharp barks. When you hear that, roll up into as tight a ball as you can and cover your eyes and ears. Then, as soon as you hear the explosion, it’s right back through the hole to the inside of your cell. There should be a large sinkhole right in the middle of the pen. Pick out a great spot to break your fall and jump. There'll be people down below to tell you what to do next."

"And how about you, Moose?" Killer asks, worry showing all over his face. "There's no way you can get through this fence to follow me. How will you keep from getting captured by the cops?"

"Don't worry about me, Killer. As soon as I know you're clear, I'm shooting straight for a break we've made in the perimeter fence. Big enough for me, but a human would struggle to get even an arm through. Should only take me about ten, fifteen seconds, then I'll be outside this prison looking in. We've got a rendezvous point already picked out, and we'll all meet up there within five minutes of the blast. You got that? Any last questions? Remember, three barks, then tuck into a ball."

"No. Yes. I mean, three barks, then tuck. I got it." Killer looks up at me, his scrunched-up face instantly softening. “Moose, buddy, I don’t know how to thank you…”

“You can thank me plenty on the other side, Killer. But right now, we got a job to do.”

Killer's Cell, 8:31 p.m.

The three barks are so loud they startle me. That's happening more and more lately, and I can't tell you how much I look forward to this entire operation being over so I can just stretch out and enjoy a regular dog's life in the suburbs. What the humans call the dog's days of summer.

I check Killer, and he's already in position, so I quickly roll up into a ball behind him, using his body as a shield to give me a little bit more protection from the blast. I know, it sounds selfish, but if Killer gets hit he gets hit, and at any rate, if that happens he's gonna need me fully functional to help deal with the sticky aftermath. Though I'm not completely sure what comes after math.

They're supposed to give us ten seconds, so I start a quiet countdown to myself. One one thousand. Two one thousand. I get all the way to seven one thousand when a sound like ten thousand dogs barking all at once splits the air and a violent, hot wind washes over us, knocking me on my back. I've had my ears covered, but even through my paws the noise was loud enough to have them ringing like church bells in a hurricane.

"Killer, you okay?" I call out, but my voice sounds all mushy in my head, like I'm wearing pillow earmuffs. I squeeze my eyes open, but there's so much dust and dirt floating in the air I can barely see past my front paw. I try a tentative sniff to see if I can locate him, but the effort just sucks all that muck up into my nose from the debris-filled air and sets me off into a racking cough. By the time I finally get my breath back the air has cleared enough to see that Killer is already gone. He's made it back through the hole in his cell, back to the inside where the explosion has opened up an escape tunnel out of the prison!

Killer's Cell, 8:42 p.m.

I let out two loud barks, as planned, and shoot around the side of his cell, heading for my own escape hole. But as I come alongside the front of Killer's cell I can see him just standing there, looking down.

"Killer! What's wrong?" I hit my brakes and skid for a second on the wet grass. "Jump, Killer! Jump!"

He just stands there looking down, shaking his head. I run back to his cell and look down at the escape tunnel myself, trying to figure out what the heck is happening. And it isn't there. There's no hole in his cell.

Killer's Cell, 8:43 p.m.

I'm standing there, staring at the solid concrete floor at Killer's feet, completely dumbstruck, when I hear voices behind me. Turning, I see Antonio and Jacques headed my way at full speed. Even though I had already given them the all clear signal, they must have figured it out, too. Something has gone terribly wrong with the plan. And I am under no illusions that that something has a name. Pops.

Killer is just standing in the middle of his cell, staring at the floor and muttering "There's no hole. There's no hole," over and over again. Antonio and Jacques finally arrive, completely out of breath. In the distance I can already hear sirens.

"What happened?" Antonio gasps between breaths.

I shrug my shoulders. "Don't know, Antonio. Obviously the bomb went off as planned, and judging by the amount of noise and all the dirt flying in the air, there should be a giant hole somewhere nearby leading down into the sewer tunnel. But since it's clearly not here, where in the heck could it be?"

Just then we hear a sound coming from the cell blocks well behind us, in the vicinity of where the Irish Retriever had been penned up earlier in the day.

"Faith and Begorrah!" he shouts out. "Get yore blarney butts over here, laddies!"

All together the three of us turn and sprint as fast as we can in that direction, leaving Killer still locked away behind us. As we get to where Red's standing, he's already pointing to a huge hole just in front of his cell.

"Thank the good Lard I was out back when it went off, or I'd be joinin' me sainted mother about now!" he tells us, rubbing one paw vigorously over his brow. "Thought it might be the Protestants fer a moment there, I'll have to tell ya. Thought the Troubles had tracked me down even out here."

I leave Antonio and Jacques to calm him down and trot over to where the hole has opened up, the edges still unstable and crumbling away into the darkness below.

“Hallo!” I yell down the hole, hoping nobody got seriously hurt when the bomb went off. After all, it was a whole lot bigger than we had ever anticipated, no pun intended.

“That you, Moose?” comes a voice from way below. “It’s Tommy. Everything okay up there? Where’s your buddy?”

I suck in a deep breath, relieved to hear his voice. “Tommy! We’re okay. But there’s been a slight problem. The hole is in the wrong place.”

“The wrong place?” Tommy calls back, and I can make out a long string of words I sometimes hear when my master does something like drop a can of my dog food on his foot. Or that time I got bored and thought his brand new Italian leather dress shoes were actually a treat for me. One word I did make out quite clearly was the name Pops.

But all the cussing and fussing isn’t going to change a thing at this point. We’ve opened up a great escape route out of the prison, but it isn’t going to do us one lick of good because Killer is still locked up tight as a tick in his prison cell, not twenty feet away. And I know a thing or two about licks and ticks.

The sirens are getting closer, and I know we're rapidly running out of time. Now that the humans are on to us, there's no way we'll be able to try this trick a second time, even if we had another bomb to try it with. Which we don't. I turn to Antonio, and he's got a sour look on his face, like he's back at home and his master's cousins have shown up for the weekend and brought their dogs. A feeling both dogs and cats can pretty much all appreciate.

At this point it seems we're out of options. If we don't beat a hasty retreat we'll all be joining Killer in the lockup pretty quickly. And who knows what the humans will have in mind for three animals that have been caught blowing a hole in their prison trying to help a wanted murderer escape. At best we'll see life. At worst that life will be very short.

Antonio shakes his head and points one claw over his shoulder toward the hole in the fence. I nod, agreeing, and I'm just about to make a bolt for it when Jacques speaks up.

"*Alors, mon amis*. I have an idea. A good friend of mine got in some trouble and wound up in Joliet a while back. There was this fire, and the firefighters, they could not free all the animals in time, so some of the dogs… you know…"

"Yeah, we know," Antonio shoots back, alternating his attention between the front of the prison and our escape route out the back. "So how does this help us here, Jacques? We can't start a fire. And even if we could, so what?"

"I am just saying, look at the locks on these cells. They are electronique, *n'est pas*? These are the locks the prisons were forced to put in to save the pets after the Joliet fire, *mais oui*?"

I look up, and he's right. They *are* the new electronic locks. Locks that open automatically whenever the fire alarm goes off. But I can't see how that helps us here. We got no way of starting a fire before the humans get here and take command of the situation. Which is gonna to happen any second now.

Antonio appears to have come to the same conclusion I have, because he's motioning for me to abandon the mission and make our escape, but Jacques holds up a paw, stopping him. Which is no small feat, given the rather impressive size of Antonio and the relatively tiny size of Jacques' French Chihuahua paw.

"Look, Fat Tony! The alarm!"

He's pointing to a little square box hanging on the wall not thirty feet away. I can just make out a tiny picture of a fire embossed on a handle that's set dead in the middle of it. I look back at Jacques, who's miming using his paw to pull down on the handle.

"Fat Tony! Grab the handle and PULL!"

Antonio's eyes shift back and forth. Once. Twice. Then suddenly he seems to make up his mind as he turns and runs as fast as he can toward the fire alarm. When he gets just five feet away he pulls up his paws sharply, flinging his massive body down toward the ground for a brief moment, then immediately he shoves back as hard as he can against the concrete, sending him flying into the air. As I'm watching him I see the back door to the guardhouse suddenly pop open, and humans in blue uniforms and badges pour out through the door, spotting us instantly and quickly leaping off the steps to race our way.

I look back at Antonio, and my first thought is he'll never make it. He's just too *big*, and as I do the quick calculations in my head I can tell right away that he's gonna fall short of the alarm.

But then at the last second he does a strange little twist in the air, dropping his right paw to his side and reaching over his head with his left foreleg, which seems to grow to impossible proportions. Then, just before he hits the wall he pops out all four of the claws on his left paw. Two claws miss the mark, but the last two latch on and Antonio holds on to the handle for dear life, his thirty or so pounds slamming against the wall with a wet *smack*. Even with all this the fire alarm handle stays locked in place. The cops are almost on us and I drop to one knee to say a quick and desperate prayer. *Our God in doggy heaven. Hallowed be her name. Our masters say come!, but our will be done, on earth as it is in heaven.*

Just then I hear Jacques let out a loud bark. "*Sacré bleu!* It worked!" And then the alarms went off, and the gates to doggy heaven sprang open.

Inside Southside Prison, 8:57 p.m.

One copper has a belly so big his belt is almost completely covered over in front, and a bald head lined with so many layers it looks like it's melting. He tries to grab for me, but I dart between his legs and out the other side, planting a paw against the leg of another copper to push off hard and to the left, toward Antonio. He's pulled in his last two claws by now and has dropped to the ground. All around us cages are springing free and the inmates, hesitating for just a brief moment in all the chaos, finally leap out onto the walkways between the cells. The humans are clearly confused, a few of them grabbing for any dog they can possibly reach and others yelling into their radios for backup.

Jacques catches my eye, pointing to the open hole down into the sewer. "Moose! The Great Escape, *mais oui*?"

I get his point instantly, and turn to Antonio, grabbing him lightly by the fur on his chest to get his attention. "I need to find Killer, get him down into the tunnel. Meanwhile, Antonio, this is our chance to save as many lives as we can. You and Jacques try to get this crowd directed back down in the hole. I'll distract the cops and work my way back to Death Row."

Antonio nods at me, then leans in closer. It's getting harder and harder to hear anything in all this bedlam, with the dogs all barking and the humans screaming out orders and obscenities at the top of their lungs. "Okay. I'll try to handle things on this end. But Moose—" He gives me a hard look. "No hero stuff, okay? Find Killer and let's blow this pop stand."

"You got it!" I take a second to try and make some kind of order out of all the mania swarming around me. One cop seems to be more in control of the situation than the others, and I know I have to take him out quickly, before he can do any damage. It's the fat cop I saw when all of this first went upside down on us. I dodge a Samoyed racing headlong into nowhere in particular, then set my sights on Officer McFatty. He's wearing leather boots that reach halfway up his thigh, halfway being the magic word. I take a few quick steps in his direction and make a leap of faith, flying through the air and sticking my landing with all four of my canine teeth sunk deeply into that upper thigh.

The Great Escape, 9:09 p.m.

McFatty is thrashing around wildly, trying to dislodge me, but I'm hanging on for the ride. He wacks my muzzle once or twice, like that's gonna have any effect, then he reaches down and pulls out a pistol, a large gun, yellow and all plasticy looking. I'm starting to have a bad feeling about all this again when he points the gun directly at my head and pulls the trigger.

I figure now is a great time to move on to Plan B, and so suddenly I let go. I can feel the needles from the gun brush within a hair's breadth of my nose as I fly off his leg and land shakily on all four paws just over a foot away. McFatty lets out a scream that would curdle mother's milk and collapses to the ground, flopping like a fish, the prongs from the Taser sticking out of his leg like needles from an African veterinarian on safari.

McFatty has now drawn the full attention of all the other cops in the area, and they immediately drop whoever or whatever they're chasing and race to help him. That gives me a clear opening to dart right through the middle of them toward Death Row.

I find Killer and the other Pits clustered in front of their open cages, free now but befuddled as to what they should do next. By their nature they're reluctant to head in the direction of the heavily armed humans blocking them from their path to freedom, and having just escaped a fate worse than death by mere inches, I can't say I really blame them. But as I look back over my shoulder I can see that Antonio and Jacques are quickly organizing a sort of conga line of dogs, each of them staying well clear of the cops and dropping one by one — with just a moments hesitation — down into the sewer. Suddenly a large black shape flashes in front of me, skirting the writhing mass of canines and disappearing into a small building in the middle of the prison yard.

I turn back to Killer and his friends. "Run! Get to Antonio, he'll show you what to do!" They seem to hold back once again, so I grab Killer by the shoulders and yell into his face, "RUN!"

The Pits are on the go. I catch a quick breath and consider my next moves. Antonio and Jacques seem to have the evacuation efforts under control, but that's largely because the cops have been distracted by their fallen soldier, and I know that situation can change at any moment. That means someone's got to create another distraction to keep the humans at bay while we get everyone down in the hole and free, and I'm just starting to chew on that idea when I get a tap on my left shoulder.

I turn and come face to face with the pit bull of my nightmares, the angel of death that had been haunting the cell at the very end of Death Row. He's a good three feet high, if not four, and now that I see him in the light I notice that he isn't really black, after all, but instead has darkly mottled fur the color of an Arctic gray wolf. And, unusual for a pit bull, he has a bush of long, curly fur drooping from the top of his head and down across his front haunches, and a breath reeking of rotting flesh and who knows what else that's he's filtering through a full set of dingy orange-yellow fangs, dripping with foamy saliva.

Choppers that I'm getting an up close and personal introduction to right at this moment.

I start to back away, slowly, so I don't startle him. "Hey, look, I don't want no trouble here."

"Hey, d-u-u-u-de, no worries," he bellows out, now grinning widely at me and doing a strange little jumpy dance of some sort. "Just wanted to say thank you, brah, for doing me and my buddies a solid."

"Wha- wha-" I manage to get out. I still can't take my eyes off those eye teeth.

"Yeah, brah. You could have just saved yer friend, you know, and left all of us behind. And nobody would have blamed you, either. I mean, the situation around here's gotten pretty gnarly, you know, and a man's gotta put his own bros first, right? But instead you put everything you had into the wave, and pulled us all out of the surf at the same time. That's a real solid, and we owe you big time, brah."

He sticks out a big paw, still doing that shrugging dance of his. "Name's Breaker. You know, like the surf off of Malibu. But most folks get that all wrong, take it to mean I'm some kind of threat.

'Cause I'm a pit bull, I guess. People judge, you know? And you must be Moose, right? Killer's got nothing but high praise when it comes to you. Say's yer kinda the Big Kahona of your stretch of sand. And I think that's pretty beachin', right?"

He looks behind me to where the conga line is starting to wind down. I check the situation myself and can see that the cops have huddled and are apparently trying to devise some kind of plan. Which reminds me that I have precious little time left of my own to throw a monkey wrench into any ideas they might come up. I motion Breaker to bend down to my level.

"Say, Breaker. I got an idea that can keep the situation around here fluid for a little while longer so we can get everyone to safety. Interested in giving me a paw with that?"

Breaker nods an enthusiastic yes, so I lean in and sketch the idea out quickly in the dirt.

"That's so radical, man," Breaker suggests as he raises back up and prepares to head into the fray.

"But it'll work, fer sure. I'm in. Catch you on the other side of the break, Cap."

He gives me a quick paw bump, then bolts off at full speed toward the knot of coppers. I steel myself and race along at full tilt right behind him.

The Great Escape, 9:21 p.m.

Up ahead I can see Officer McFatty look up just in time to throw both his arms in front of his face to protect himself from the hundred plus pound ball of snarling pit bull that piles at full speed right into the mass of policemen, scattering them every which way like they were a line of bowling pins. I arrive just behind him, throwing caution to the wind and sinking my teeth indiscriminately into any flesh I can find. The humans are screaming in terror and bouncing off each other, trying to escape. Breaker spins around and comes back in a wide circle for another shot at Bowling for Coppers, his jowls pulled way back over his bared orange-yellow fangs, a low growl like a freight train in a tornado rumbling out of his chest.

I can hear Antonio and Jacques in the background, urging everyone forward amidst an incessant chorus of yelping and barking. "Let's go, people! Get a move on! Jump! Jump!" Every now and then I catch a hint of something else, like a hiss or a cat screaming out in the night. But my attention right now is almost completely focused on the humans, who have started spinning around in circles, thoroughly lost in the pandemonium, swatting at the air furiously like they're being attacked by a swarm of bees.

Suddenly I find myself ejected forcefully from the sea of blue, and pivoting quickly to get back into the action, I'm surprised to see Killer standing directly across the escape tunnel from Antonio, waving his paws to urge the crowd to keep moving in the right direction, toward freedom. Just behind him I can barely make out Ike, standing proud and black high above the surging current, directing another long line of cats out of the mysterious building I'd seen him disappear into earlier. One by one they're pressing themselves up alongside the oblivious throng of canines and down into the sewer as well. Wow. I'd forgotten all about the cat cages. And, now that I think about it, once their cages popped opened when the fire alarm went off, they'd have all been stuck behind the locked steel door closing off the feline section of the prison. If Ike hadn't shown up when he did, somehow figuring out how to pick the lock with those claws of his, they'd all still be trapped in their part of the prison, ready to be recaptured when this is all over.

But that isn't my problem right now. Other pets have stepped up and are doing their part, so I need to stay focused on my role in all of this. I can see that the humans have finally started to realize that Breaker, unlike me, isn't biting anyone. With his street cred down the toilet, it's clearly well past time for him to make his own great escape. "Breaker, Breaker, break free!" I yell out, trying to make sure he can hear me over the cacophony of voices.

He looks up, and I think I can lip read what he says before he butts one last cop in the back, flinging him forward and setting off a chain reaction of tumbling human dominos, then ducks right and heads for the tunnel. *Good surfin', brah... Catch ya on the next wave.*

The place is rapidly emptying out, but we still have a few dozen more stragglers to save before we can call it a day. Plus, of course, the A Team. What we're calling Antonio's Team.

With Breaker out of the picture, the humans are starting to regroup, and I can hear more sirens heading our way in the distance. We've got minutes at best before we're overwhelmed with the riot squad. Maybe even the SWAT team. I gotta stop and think. I look up and see McFatty standing with the other coppers, working out some kind of plan. His back's to me, which is his big mistake. I lick my lips to make sure they're nice and moistened, then put my legs into high gear once again and head in his direction like a thoroughbred stallion on his final push for the finish line. Although, to be honest, to anyone else watching it might have looked a little less dramatic. But hey, it's the only gear I've got.

When I reach McFatty he's still totally unaware that I'm right behind him. But that's gonna change, and fast. I leap as high into the air as I possibly can, the wind singing through my open muzzle, and clamp down with all four canines right in the middle of his doughy fat rump.

He lets out a sound like a thousand piglets squealing for their mommas at supper time and starts strutting and flailing his arms backward, trying to knock me off. But he's got so much blubber around his middle that he can't possibly get those flopping arms much past his sides, and he winds up looking like he's trying to do some kind of funky chicken dance.

I've got both eyes trained on the action around me, and as he spins around, his friends — who were confused at first about his dance moves, and a few have actually started to join in — finally realize what's happening and try to grab me to pull me off him. Now, I don't want to brag, but pit bulls and German Shepherds got nothin' on an Aussie when it comes to clamping on strength, and my four canines are easily over an inch in length, but I gotta worry about the funky chicken turning into more of a Kentucky Fried Chicken, with them winding up holding onto some of my wings and thighs. Knowing that discretion is the better part of valor, at the last possible moment I give up on riding his tail, sliding down one of his legs all the way to the ground like it's a fire pole, then try a little Gale Sayers action in and out of their ankles. If you don't know who Gale Sayers is, then you're clearly not a Chicago Bears fan. Best running back ever, and you Cleveland Brownies can just forget all your crazy talk about Jim Brown.

So, anyway, now I'm back on all fours. I shoot free of the copper love fest, yapping for all I'm worth, and head back in the general direction of Death Row, away from the getaway route and the safety of all my friends.

The humans have given up on the escaping dogs and are now focusing all of their attention on me. It's McFatty out front, yelling and moving much faster than I'd ever give him credit for, considering his size. "That there's the gall darned cur what bit me! Git 'em boys!"

I consider swinging around to the back of the cell block, but that would only give them a chance to cut me off at the pass. At the last minute I cut inside, instead, juking at a ninety degree angle that the coppers try to match and fail epically, crashing into one another and collapsing into a huge blue ball of flesh behind me. I use the opportunity to open up a lead, rounding the lap dog cells and heading straight for the now-empty cat cages.

The humans have regrouped and are once again in full pursuit. Just then the guardhouse door flies open and even more humans join the chase, not bothering to stop for even a second to properly evaluate the situation on the ground. That's a human for you, always acting with their gut instincts and almost never with their brains. Unlike us dogs.

But I'm not complaining. I can see out of the corner of my eye that the last of the inmates are now disappearing down the hole, and Antonio is sending me a silent question, asking if I need him to help out with the chase. I shake my head no, still in full stride, and before I make it to the bend taking me around the east side cell block I can just catch the sight of him dropping down into the hole himself, followed right behind by Killer, Jacques and Ike.

Now I've got a decision to make. I can try to circle back to the escape tunnel myself, but with all the humans pouring in through the front gates there's a good chance at least a few of them might wise up to what's going on and cut me off. My second choice is the hole through the back fence. I risk a glance back over my shoulder and see that two of the coppers have pulled out their yellow guns. I've run out of time to try the old eenie meenie miny moe trick, I've just got to pick one path and commit to it. So back fence hole it is.

I knock a rake loose from where it's resting against a cell block wall and start to weave a little right and left as I head for the exit. And I'm quickly glad I did, as I can hear a couple of *phht* sounds just behind me and can see the darts from the yellow guns just missing me on either side. Suddenly one of the shooters must have stepped on the rake that I dropped in passing, because I hear a loud *whack* and the darts go silent for the moment.

Max is at the fence just up ahead of me, barking furiously, egging me on. With all this chasing around back and forth, my gas gage is well past empty, and by now I'm running on fumes. I just have a few more feet to go and then I'm free — but then I feel what must be a human hand sweep across the curly hairs on the back of my tail, trying to get a grip, and I know there are others where that came from. In the far distance I can still hear Officer McFatty screaming something obscene at the top of his lungs, but he has clearly fallen well behind the crowd at some point during the chase and is no longer anything I need to worry about.

I'm just barely managing to drag one paw in front of the other when suddenly a blurry shape shoots out of the hole in the fence and blasts right past me, almost brushing my left side as it flies by. Behind me I can hear a new strain of cussing, then someone yelling "Catch that Corgi" and "She's nipped me!" Just a foot from the fence I finally collapse, my legs going numb and useless underneath me like they're landing gear folding up into an airplane. I slide about half the way to the hole, then a powerful paw reaches out, grabs me by the collar and pulls me all the rest of the way through the fence.

"Moose! You okay?" Max is crouching over me, deep creases standing out all over his forehead.

"Yeah. I'm okay," I manage to choke out, my chest heaving up and down like there's an alien in there trying to break out. Somehow I get the energy to roll over on my side, and through the hole in the fence and my still blurry eyes I can barely make out some familiar-looking little blonde and white dog racing in and out among the feet of the humans, nipping at their heels and quickly herding them into a tight knot.

"Bella!" shouts Max. "He's safe! Moose is safe! Get outa there, you crazy little Corgi!"

Bella? It's Bella that came to save me, just then at the last moment? My eyes start to refocus, and now I can see her, giving one of the coppers a final nip for good measure, then turning and sprinting our way, her long tail curled tightly up over her back and her hind legs locked into that little rabbit hop she always reserves for when she needs to truck along at full speed. In a heartbeat she's through the hole, just in front of a human arm that appears suddenly from out of nowhere into our side of the fence, grasping blindly for anything it can reach. Bella turns back gamely and plants another small nip on its hand, and the arm disappears with a yelp.

Max has my collar in his teeth and is swinging me up over on his back. "Hang on, little fella!" he yells. "We gotta make tracks. They got guns!"

He leaps forward down the fence line, somehow blending into the grass and weeds growing up along the fence like he's some kind of ghost. Bella is right behind us, running just as fast as she possibly can and grinning furiously. In just minutes we're clear of the prison and winding our way through a small forest, heading toward the rendezvous point.

Rendezvous Point, 10:07 p.m.

As we pull into the clearing, there are so many different breeds milling around it almost looks like a show at the Kennel Club. That is, if the Club allowed any cats to join as members. I wonder if cats have a Kennel Club of their own?

Anyway, riding on Max's shoulders at high speed has been an exhilarating experience, but I'm finally starting to catch my breath from all of the drama back at the prison. And I've still got quite a bit of an adrenalin boost rushing through my veins, which I know is going to make things pretty painful for me when it all wears down. As is my right rear leg, which evidently got wrenched out of place at some point during that final dash for the fence line.

Speaking of which, Bella has been staying right behind us all the way to the rendezvous point, and is now sidling up beside Max, looking around as well at all of the dogs and cats filling up the small clearing.

"Bella," I manage to croak out.

She looks up at me, a scowl sweeping across her face. "Well, if it isn't Joe Hero, Luke Skywalker of the Chicago South Side, taking on the whole Empire single-handedly. I thought you promised me you wouldn't do anything stupid. Wouldn't risk your life on some fool mission."

"Bella, I—" I start to explain.

"No, I get it, Moose. It's a guy thing, always charging into the middle of things without thinking. Forgetting that you have people at home who need you just as much as these strangers you think you're protecting. People at home who love you very much, whose hearts would absolutely break right in two if anything ever happened to your sorry little Yorkie butt."

I know that she's just baiting me with the Yorkie thing to try and get under my skin, but as I look down at her pleadingly, I can see her scowl start to soften. I understand what's got her tail up over her back. I scared her. Really, really bad. Heck, I scared myself, for that matter. If any single one of those humans had gotten a good grip on my collar, I'd have been toast. But I wasn't worried about any of that at the time it all went down. I just wasn't thinking about the risk. And she's right about that, too.

"Bella, I really can't say anything other than I'm sorry. I'm sorry for any pain I've caused you, for making you worry about me, for breaking my promise. But hey, at least give me some credit. The situation on the ground was a bit *dynamic*. We had no way of knowing Pops was going to screw up the placement of the bomb. If in fact he did — who knows if anyone could have done any better? But I wasn't the only one who put his life on the line for his friends tonight. Killer was there. And Ike. And Antonio and Jacques, both of whom really knew none of us all that well before this weekend, had nothing at all to gain by taking on the risk. The danger."

I pause to catch my breath, then go for the big sell. "And, by the way, if anyone's going to be mad about everything that happened tonight, I seem to recall telling you in no uncertain terms to stay put back at headquarters. But then all of a sudden you're right out there in the middle of the prison yard, saving my fur. So who's the big hero now, eh? Seems to me, if someone's gonna be the unsung hero, it's my little Corgi Porgi, here." I drop down off of Max's back and try to engulf her in a huge hug. And as hard as I try, my Aussie arms barely make it halfway around her substantial chest.

"You know, Moose," she tells me, pushing away at first but then finally caving in and draping her arms loosely around my scruffy neck. "You are totally incorrigible. You hear that? Totally incorrigible."

Rendezvous Point, 10:31 p.m.

The escapees are still filtering in by ones and twos from the tunnel, and I spy Tommy Tuxedo flitting about from one side of the clearing to the other like he's a Papillon himself, leading the recovery effort. I excuse myself from Bella and head that way. I got something important Tommy and I need to discuss.

"Hey Tommy!" He turns and sees me immediately.

"Moose! Glad to see you made it out alive. Last word I got from these guys, it was nip and tuck for you back there."

"Yeah, well, it'll be a fine day in cat country when a human can ever outsmart an Aussie, that's for sure," I tell him. "But Tommy, got a minute? Something I need to get straight with you."

Tommy looks concerned, thinking maybe I'm angry at him for something, but he points out a quiet spot over near the edge of the clearing and we head that way.

"What's eatin' you Moose?" he asks when we're finally alone.

"Well, it's nothing major, it's just something that came to me back at the prison yard when I was having a kind of conversation with that big pit bull, Breaker."

"Yeah, what's that?" Tommy asks, relaxing a little.

"It has to do with Pops. I caught your look, back when we were first setting the bomb. Neither of us thought he got it right. We both thought the sound was coming from further back in the tunnel."

"Yeah, and it turns out we were right," Tommy agrees. "The truth is, the old boy's hearing just isn't what it used to be, and we were both pretty stupid not to pick up on all the clues back then when we should have. Turned this whole operation from a simple blow and grab into a complete cluster truck. We're just lucky it all turned out as well as it did."

"Right," I explain. "And that's the thing. Just between the two of us, we know what really went down in the sewer tunnel, how Pops messed it all up.

But the rest of these guys have absolutely no idea. Oh sure, Antonio and the rest of the A Team know about the original plan, but what if we hand them all a slightly modified version of what really happened down there? An alternative facts version, if you will?"

"What are you proposing, Moose?"

"I'm just saying, instead of making Pops out to look like a complete fool, why don't we let him go down as some kind of hero here, himself? Make it look like he came up with the idea to save all of the dogs and cats in the prison, instead of just Killer, all on his own? So then he picks out this great new location for the blast, right in the center of the prison complex, instead of inside of Killer's cell?"

Tommy chews the idea over for a few seconds, then finally nods, his lips bending upward from a deep frown to a wry little smile. "I like the way you think, Moose. Instead of trying to embarrass the old guy, we turn the whole blasted thing into a big celebration of his life. And why not? In some ways, it also spills over into the lives of all the other dogs and cats we saved tonight. Instead of their freedom being just some freak accident, all just the result of a stupid mistake by some old geezer, now it's an act of divine mercy. Of God shining down on them and giving them all a second chance." He's rubbing his chin, thinking. "You really got something there, Moose. I can work with this. Thanks."

"Hey, don't thank me," I tell him. "Thank Breaker, he's the one who gave me the idea. By the way, speaking of pits, have you seen Killer since the breakout?"

"Yeah, he's over there in that line on the other side of the compound, waiting for his dechipping."

Once I know where to look, he's hard to miss. "Okay, thanks Tommy. And I'll circle back with everyone else to make sure they're all on board with this."

"Sure thing," Tommy says. "Oh, and one last thing, Moose?"

I'm already on my way over to Killer, but I stop in my tracks and turn around.

"Thanks for everything you did back there. None of this would have worked if it hadn't been for you. You're just about the bravest Yorkie this world has ever seen."

"Yorkie?" I start to protest. "Why, I—" I stop myself in mid sentence. Now is not the time for any of that. Definitely the wrong time, given how we all worked so hard tonight as one species, one breed to save each other's fur. Not to mention Tommy and Antonio and all the other cats. "I — I didn't do anything anybody else wouldn't have done in my place, Tommy. But — thanks. I think we all showed a lot of courage out there on that field tonight. And underground, setting the bomb and then dodging all the cave-ins from up above, and meanwhile keeping the line moving. We made a great team tonight, all of us. And hopefully some great friendships, as well."

"Yeah, a truly great team it was, Moose. The greatest. But, you know, maybe we were a little too quick on the trigger with the whole A Team thing. Maybe we should think about changing that, given what all went down tonight. I'm thinking, going forward, history should probably know us all as the M Team, instead. What do you say?"

I smile back at him, touched by the unexpected compliment, as I disappear into the shadows on my way over to check in with Killer. And the conversation with him I'd pay any amount of kibble not to have.

Dechipping Line, 10:59 p.m.

I catch up with Killer just as he's arrived at the front of the line. An old bloodhound named Bob is sniffing out the location of the ID chips on the dogs' backsides, and Fisheye is there with his incredibly long and razor sharp claw, digging them all out. I watch quietly and not without a little horror as they perform the delicate operation on Killer, but to my surprise the whole thing goes pretty smoothly and, considering what's at stake, rather painlessly.

"Aren't you worried about the wound site getting infected?" I ask Fisheye as Killer hops down off the table, a table they've evidently dragged up from deep inside the sewer tunnel.

"Nah," Fisheye answers, his eyes still a little lopsided and throwing off my balance a bit. "We just have 'em lick it clean a couple of times a day. Dog saliva is the *mas bueno* antiseptic around. If the humans weren't so all-fired focused on the Amazon rain forest, looking for fancy cures in curare and toad toxins, they might realize they've got a gold mine here right under their feet." He points to his next patient, a long-haired miniature Dachshund. "In some cases, quite literally under foot." The Dachshund, with a truly valiant effort, finally manages to crawl up on the table. "Hey look, *jefe*, I'd love to talk, but—" Fish motions to the long line of dogs still waiting to be seen, and I just smile, tap a paw on his shoulder for support and head off to catch up with Killer.

"So, big buddy, I noticed you held back from getting the heck out of Dodge back there, and instead stayed to help out with the rescue."

"Yeah." Killer hangs his head a bit. He's a dog of few barks, and gets uncomfortable anytime the conversation veers anywhere close to his feelings. "Kinda thought, you know, pay it forward and all that. Truth is, I'd already kinda given up on life. Kinda gave up on everything when I saw Penny lying like that in the road, bleeding. So when all this happened tonight, I thought, hey, maybe it's a sign, you know? Maybe it's not supposed to be my time to go. Maybe I'm destined to do something good in this world, after all. So, God gave me a second chance —

you guys gave me a second chance — and, like, I figure I gotta do something with it. So when I got to the escape tunnel, and that big fat cat was yelling 'Jump,' there was like a voice inside my head that said 'Not yet.' Does any of that make sense to you?"

Actually, it all made perfect sense. Most of us waltz through our lives, and it's all about kibbles and bits and chew sticks and the occasional walkies, and what does any of that mean, really? When it comes your time to be put down, what in the long term is anyone ever gonna really remember about you? Is even your family gonna remember all that much when they've got a new puppy in the house peeing on all the rugs and chewing on the furniture?

"That's really deep, Killer," I tell him. "I think you might just have a future as a dog philosopher."

We walk along in silence for a few more minutes when the question finally comes up. Killer stops and looks at me directly, intensely, eye to eye. Not something I can recall him ever doing before. Then he squeaks out just one word. "Penny?"

I can't maintain the eye contact. Not right now. I turn and keep walking along the path, slowly. "Yeah. She — she didn't make it, Killer. But the docs said she didn't suffer," I lie.

It takes him a few more minutes to get out the second question. "Why?"

It's amazing to me how much emotional content he can load into these one word questions. At least they're emotional for me. Once again, I struggle to come up with just the right answer.

"I — I wish I could say there was some big reason why she had to be taken from us that night, Killer, some big mystery, something she did that brought her to that end. But the truth is, Penny just happened to be in the wrong place at the wrong time, that's all. It was just a random, senseless killing, something that's happening all too often these days in Chicago. You know, it's not all that different from when someone gets run over crossing the road. It just happens. God makes a space for you in Doggy Heaven, and then it's your turn. Your reward. But at least Antonio and I tracked down the guy who did it.

And he got his reward, too. And — trust me — he didn't wind up in Doggy Heaven."

A few more minutes passed, and then the third and final question. "Who?"

I shake my head and reach over to lay a paw on his shoulder while we're walking. "Don't know his name. Doesn't matter, really. Just some young punk. Some gangbanger. In a way, his life was thrown away, too, just like Penny's. A waste. But Killer—"

We stop, and face each other again. He gives me a hard look, but I can still see the tears forming in his eyes in the dark. "Killer, the thing is, Penny isn't really gone. She's still watching over you, up there in heaven. And she is still very much alive, right here." I touch his heart with my paw. "And right here." I move my paw up to touch the side of his head. "As long as you remember her, as long as you remember the love the two of you shared, she'll never be truly gone. She'll be right here, living all the time inside of you."

Killer nods his head for a second, then turns away. I can hear the tears in his voice as he heads off further into the darkness to be alone with his thoughts. “Thank you, Moose, for saving me. And not just from the prison. You’re the best friend a pit bull could ever have.”

I stand for a moment and watch him go. I know that tonight, he just needs to find some way to heal, to put this whole ugly story behind him, to keep moving forward. And tomorrow is when we’ll start that new journey together. A journey to a much brighter future. But for me, the night is unfortunately still very young.

Refugee Camp, 12:43 a.m.

The rendezvous point was originally intended to just be a quick meet-up spot before we escaped back into the city, but now it's become a full-fledged refugee camp. As I walk among the dogs and cats sheltering in the camp, some slightly injured from their jumps into the yawning darkness of the sewer tunnel, some still nursing injuries suffered on the street before they were captured by the police, I'm touched by their appreciation for what we've done. Once again I'm reminded of how avoiding any discussion of what really happened down there in the sewer with Pops can pay huge benefits in terms of these folks' inspiration, the personal energy they're going to need to rebuild their lives and move forward.

PETSEC assures me that we can find homes for everyone. Many of the refugees are simply strays, torn from their families during a thunderstorm or some other minor catastrophe, and using the PETSEC databases and the pets' own memories we have a good chance of getting them back home again, of reuniting them with their loved ones. Some of them had been terribly abused in the past, so they'll need new homes. And some have been abused so badly it'll take many months of therapy before they're ready to deal with humans again. If at all.

But, with one exception, none of that is my problem, and even then, most of the burden of Killer's social rehabilitation is on PETSEC's shoulders, well beyond my pay grade. For now, I've only got two things to worry about. First, sleep. I haven't had a wink of sleep since all this first began, back last Friday night when Penny was murdered, and I'm so dead right now I'm about to drop in my tracks. We have a good five or six hours to kill before the L starts running again out here, so I have a good idea how I plan to kill that time. And that leads to the second thing. Going home. I know it's a risk. They'll probably make a huge effort to figure out how I've been getting out of the yard all this time, and I just can't afford to get penned up right now when I still have so much to get wrapped up for Killer. For his new life.

But before I can take care of Killer, I've got to take care of myself. I can't even think about what little Billy must be thinking right about now back home, with me being missing for two whole days. And one thing I sure can't let happen is to have them make a trip down to the pound looking for me and then come home with a brand new puppy as a substitute. No way I want to have to deal with that nightmare scenario for the next few years. I think I might just prefer to be back in prison with all the other unlucky inmates.

So now I just need to hunt down Bella and grab a little shuteye, then Antonio can help hook us up with the right trains and we can be back on our front doorsteps, wagging our tails for all we're worth, come early Monday morning. Before our masters and mistresses head off for work. It's been a long, long weekend for both of us. But it's a story we'll likely tell our grandchildren well into the future. Or, actually, Bella might. As for me, well…

Refugee Camp, 1:07 a.m.

Bella's standing pretty much right where I left her, talking about whatever to Max with her usual nonstop energy. I hang back in the shadows for a few more minutes, just watching her. I don't know when I've ever seen her look more beautiful. Or any other dog, for that matter.

Finally their conversation seems to wind down and I step out to say hi and thank them both for saving my fur tonight.

"Don't mention it, Moose," Max tells me, blushing. "I'll have to say, you were by far the biggest, meanest dog out there tonight. I was just glad I could help out a little."

Bella is giving me a curious look, so I say goodbye to Max as he heads over to where PETSEC's handing out some chew sticks and a little water.

"You know, Moose, Max is right. You really were wonderful out there, leading all those humans away from the escape tunnel, giving Fat Tony and the rest of them time to get everyone to safety."

“Aw, Bella, it weren’t nothin’,” I stammer, suddenly incapable of finding anything better to say.

“No, it was something. It was actually something pretty special. To all of us.” She’s smiling at me, but then she somehow starts to drift away from me, lost in thought.

“Everything okay, Bella?” I ask.

“Yeah, just something...” She’s rubbing a paw along her jaw line distractedly. “Moose, just how well do you know this cat, Fat Tony?”

“Antonio? Well, I met him just yesterday morning for the first time. But he seems like a swell enough guy. And he has a great reputation, especially after that Evanston thing with the Greyhounds. Why?”

“It’s just that...” She hesitates again, and I can tell that something’s eating at her.

“What is it, Bella?” I ask. “What’s bothering you?”

After a long moment she looks up at me, and I can see the concern lining her eyes and forehead. “It’s just that, the last time we were back at his office, right after lunch today, I was checking out all the pictures and stuff he had hanging on the walls. You know, typical wall of honor stuff, right? But the thing is, Fat Tony wasn't in a single picture. Not one. Just some bald headed human with glasses. And all of the diplomas and awards? None of them said Antonio whatever. Every single one of them had just one name on it. Michael Shapiro. Ever heard of him?"

I think back. Hard. But the truth is, I'm not very good with names. Especially human names. I mean, I got my mistress down, Helen, but since she's the one who always feeds me morning, noon and night, I better not miss that one. And I think my other human is Gary something or other. But I wouldn't bet any kibble on that.

"Michael Cheerios? No, that doesn't seem to ring any bells for me." As I mention the word bells, once again I start salivating out of control. Seems to always happen to me, and for the life of me I can't figure out why. Maybe I should take that up with Dr. May the next time I see him—

Bella looks exasperated, fidgeting absent-mindedly with her collar. "No, not cheerios. *Shapiro.* Honestly, Moose—"

She gets that lost in space look again, and her tail is starting to curl up tight against her back. A sure sign she's chewing on something that doesn't taste right. I decide to try and lighten the mood a little. "So, whatever his name is, who cares what's hanging on Antonio's walls? Maybe he got it all in a garage sale or something." I once made off with this totally awesome teddy bear from a garage sale down the street, already had a small rip in it, and within an hour the whole living room looked like a snowstorm hit it. One of my best days ever.

But the daydreaming look is gone, and now Bella looks stern, almost angry. Or maybe it's just gas. It's always hard to tell with dogs.

"Moose, you need to be serious for a moment. This is important. I don't think Fat Tony has been completely honest with us. I think he's hiding something."

"You mean like a rib bone out in the yard?" I suggest. "Do cats even do that?"

"No, not a rib bone." She stands up and moves my way, laying a paw gently on the side of my face. "Moose, normally I think your naivety is all pretty endearing. It's part of what makes you so loveable to everyone. To me. But I'm telling you, Fat Tony has a big secret he's keeping really close to the vest. And someday that secret might come back to bite us in the butt."

I can't remember ever seeing Antonio wearing a vest, but I think I get what she's saying. And I can't help but remember all those times his Italian accent has slipped off like a loose collar in a stiff wind. But standing here tonight I can't see why any of that will ever matter a handful's worth of Purina to us. The investigation is over, Killer and the other pets are free. And tomorrow is a new day. A day that no longer has Antonio in it.

"Bella, I hear ya, but I think it's all just the nervous Nellie Corgi in you coming out again. That whole bark at the butterflies thing you always have going on. Okay, so maybe Antonio isn't exactly what he says he is. Maybe he's got some secret identity he's hiding. Or maybe, just maybe you're over thinking all this, like you always do." I lay a paw softly on her cheek, and can feel her tension start to slip away. "All I know is, other than trying to figure out where I'm gonna come up with those six cans of tuna I owe him, we'll never see Antonio Gattogrosso ever again. It's been one crazy weekend, but now all that's ancient history. Old news. The only thing we really need to worry about right now is tomorrow morning, and how we're going to explain things to our humans. I bet they're worried sick about us."

Bella leans into me, her muzzle pressed close against mine. A nice feeling, if I have to say so myself. "I hope you're right, Moose. I hope this is all behind us. But I just can't shake a nagging feeling that it's not. And a sense that we're not quite finished with Fat Tony."

Hyde Park, 7:35 a.m.

The signs are stapled up everywhere, making Bella and I look like some kind of modern day canine Bonnie and Clyde. I give her a wink as we trot into the neighborhood, and she smiles and winks back. My hind leg is still throbbing from where I strained it running from the cops, but Fisheye assures me it's just a pull and it'll get better over time. I'm not all that sure I really care if it gets much better, to be honest. The limp just gives me a few more opportunities to relive our adventures over the past two days. Experiences I can bet you no other dog in Hyde Park has ever come close to, even in their best leg twitching dreams.

We get to our respective houses and say our goodbyes for now. Bella starts to turn away, then at the last minute reaches over and gives me a muzzle bump. "Later, Tiger," she purrs, just like a cat. I wonder not for the first time just how much hanging out with all these felines can rub off on a dog, anyway. But, to be completely fair, these last two days have given me a completely different perspective on our lesser pet companions, you know? They're really not all that bad, once you get to know them.

I look up at my front porch, hesitating. All the way home I've been pondering the best way to do this. Should I just crawl up into the backyard and pretend that I've been there all along? Nah, they'll never buy that, and that'll just get them searching for how I got out of the yard in the first place. I've got way too much invested in that one little rabbit hole to give it away now. And if there's anything I've picked up for sure these last forty-eight hours, it's the importance of having a good escape route.

In the end I decide to just hang out in the bushes and wait for my master to come pulling out of the garage on his way to work. So as soon as I hear the garage door go up I come racing out, spinning around in circles on my two back legs and letting out a string of arfs like I've never barked before. He stops the car instantly and jumps out.

"Helen!" he yells in the direction of the house. "Moose is back!"

The front door slams open and my mistress is down the steps in a heartbeat, with Billy right behind her.

"Mooooose!" he screams, scooping me up in his arms and spinning around in circles until I'm actually getting quite dizzy. Next door I can hear pretty much the same scenario being played out in Bella's front yard. It's gonna be a good day.

Hyde Park, Five Days Later

Everything is finally returning to some semblance of normal around the old neighborhood. Bella and I are back to our old habits — although she's wearing a shock collar for now while her humans try to figure out how she managed to escape from her back yard — and Killer is off living at some safe house while PETSEC prepares him for his new life on the lam. Or, more accurately, for some nice suburban family home they're scouting out for him.

If it wasn't for the fact that Killer's not around anymore to shoot the breeze with, I could easily imagine that nothing at all has changed, that nothing really happened last weekend. Okay, other than the fact that Bella and I seem to have this *thing* going on between us, which I'm still trying to work through. I mean, I've been a lone wolf for a long time, and I'm not all that sure I'm ready to change all that. Putting on the old ball and chain, if you catch my drift.

It's a beautiful day out, sunny but cool, just the way I like it. My humans still haven't found my rabbit hole in the back corner of my yard, so I still got my freedom to come and go, but I'm trying to keep that on the down low for now. At least while they have their antennas up for how I got out last Friday and stayed missing the whole weekend. Can't say I really blame them for that. It's actually kinda touching, in a way.

I just finished breakfast, a double helping of the good stuff — my people must think I need some fattening up after skipping out on two days worth of meals, and I'm not complaining — so I hunt down a good soft spot in the warm sun to stretch out and rest my eyes. I can hear Bella coming through her doggie door to hang out in her back yard, too, and I almost get up to say hi, but the sun feels *so* good this morning, especially after the winter we just lived through. My eyes are just starting to roll back in my head, and I'm facing down this six foot squirrel with a major attitude, an acorn grasped in both of his paws, when all of a sudden Bella's scream splits the air.

I'm up in an instant, and realize that I'm pointed the wrong way, so I spin around, my mouth open for anything and everything and my eyes sweeping across her back yard, looking for any sign of my girl Bella.

And then I see her. Some ginormous black dog has Bella by the front of her collar with his right paw and is dragging her inch by inch toward the back gate, which is now gaping wide open. After the first scream she's gone silent, the collar and his knuckles digging deep into her throat, shutting off her windpipe. It takes me a second or so to make sense of the situation. That dog, the one that's got her. I know him. He's one of the CC's that captured Antonio and me and had us tied up back at CC headquarters. It's Ralfie.

I'm at the side fence in a heartbeat. "Let her go, you stupid animal!" I spit out. "Let her go or I swear to Doggie Heaven I'll split you limb from limb!"

Ralfie has stopped just inside the gate, and is staring back at me, a malevolent leer spreading slowly across his face. “Tough words from such a little dog. Why don’t you come over here and show me what you got, Yorkie?”

“Let her go!” I bark at him at full throttle. “You got a problem, it’s with me! She’s got nothing to do with anything that’s happened between us!”

“Yeah, well, sometimes you need to drop a little bait in the water to catch the right fish,” he sneers at me. “And speakin’ of which, where’s that big ugly fat feline you were snooping around with the other night? The one with the pointy hair? I’m still thinkin’ you two owe me a meal, if you know wut I mean.”

Bella’s face is starting to turn a dark shade of blue, and I know I’ve got to think of something pretty quick to break her loose. I realize it’s a suicide move, but I got no choice but to take this brute of a Doberman on. With any luck I can keep him busy long enough for Bella to get someplace safe, someplace he can’t follow. Throwing caution to the wind, I dart for the alley through my hole in the fence, still keeping both eyes trained on Ralfie and my girl.

Once I'm out in the alley, I confront Ralfie, slowly, growling from deep in my belly and showing every tooth I've got. He's still just laughing at me and dragging Bella kicking and — I wish — screaming right behind him. I can see I've only got seconds now, a minute at the most to free her before it's too late.

Just then Ralfie steps through the gate, grinning like a banshee, and then, without any warning, lets out a bloodcurdling scream that would have had me peeing my pants if I'd been wearing any, instantly dropping Bella's collar like it's a rib bone straight off the barbecue. "What the—"

It's the shock collar, I suddenly realize. It went off in his paw when he stepped through the gate. And it's the one chance I need to spring Bella free.

Ralfie's still shaking his right paw violently in the air when I hit him at full speed, my canines sinking deep into his exposed left ankle. As my body slams around to the other side I can hear something *snap*, and since I'm apparently still in one piece I assume I'm not the one that's broken.

"My leg!" he screams, dropping to one knee and reaching for his ankle. "You're gonna suffer for this, you stupid, worthless mutt! You're gonna pay for this!"

I let go of his leg and roll to a stop, then quickly jump back on all four paws, shaking as I reassess the situation. "Bella, get to my hole!" I holler between breaths. "Run! Get inside! Get Helen!"

She takes off, rabbit hopping her way through my escape tunnel, then in a flash darting across my yard and slamming through my private doggie door. I spin around and see Ralfie rising up not a foot or so in front of me. And apparently he's not all that happy to see me.

His jowls pull back and I'm looking into a mouth that could have fit on a fully adult Tyrannosaurus Rex. Like greased lightning on a rail he flings those fangs straight at my fully exposed back, and only by twisting my entire torso in mid air do I barely manage to dodge them in time, shooting between his back legs and planting another quick nip on his injured ankle as I fly past. Just in case he'd forgotten.

I hear him scream again just inches behind me, so I try the whole left-right shuffle step I used to escape the prison, working hard to throw off his aim. I know I'm just about out of moves when suddenly I hear my mistress's voice call out from inside the kitchen behind me.

"Bella! What in the world are you doing in my kitchen? And why are you barking at the doggie door, dear?"

I go left when I should have gone the other way, and suddenly he's got me solid by the tip end of my right ear. Nothing I can do about that now, so I make the sacrifice and roll hard left. I can hear more than feel the searing pain of flesh tearing off my ear, but at least I'm free.

Helen's voice calls out again, this time louder. She's in the back yard!

"Oh my stars! You horrible creature! What are you doing to my Moose!"

By the early morning shadow he's throwing I can see Ralfie hesitate in his pursuit for just a moment, thrown off by Helen's comment. And that single moment is all I need. I use his hesitation to open up a small but critical gap, swinging around him in a wide arc, heading for my hole, ignoring the pain shooting from my ear and my injured right leg. But it only takes a moment before he's on to me once again. I shoot through the rabbit hole at top speed, hoping I'm free. But he doesn't bother with the hole, and instead sinks down on his haunches and clears the fence in one long leap. I plant a paw to cut sharply to the left, but I'm way too late with that move and he falls like a Martian meteor right out of the sky on top of me, crushing the air from my lungs and laying me out flat.

I'm done for. I squeak out one last "I love you, Bella" and prepare for my fate. It'll only take one quick, brutal bite from those jaws and I'm toast.

But the moment passes and somehow I'm still alive. Ralfie eases up just a hint and I manage to roll out from under him. Suddenly I sense more than see a dark shape flying through the air toward us.

Whack! “You filthy beast!” Helen is yelling. “You leave my Moosie alone!” *Whack! Whack, whack!*

I gather my resources and scoot a few feet further away, and look back to see my mistress pummeling the life out of Ralfie with the business end of a giant broom.

Whack, whack! “You want some more of this, mister Doberman?” she’s yelling. “Why, I have a right mind to—”

There’s one final, ear splitting *whack*, and suddenly Ralfie is back on his feet and headed lickety split for the fence, Helen right on his heels. He clears it again in one giant leap and is running like his tail is on fire and his paws are a’catchin’, straight down our alley and out toward the street. Helen pauses at the back gate to make sure he’s gone for sure, then races back to my side, stroking my fur and gently examining the bloody damage to my torn right ear.

"Oh, you poor brave dear! Did you do all that to protect Bella? Oh, you poor, poor thing! Let's get you in the car and have Dr. May take a look at that ear!"

Bella is right beside us, and leans over to give my injured ear a sweet lick. It hurts like the dickens when she touches it, but no way I'm gonna tell her that. I'll gladly lose both my ears if that's what it takes to keep her safe.

Fat Tony's Office, The Next Day

Antonio is busy talking quietly on the phone. I assume it's another client, so I take advantage of the opportunity to poke around his office. As many times as I've been here in the past, I was always so distracted, so focused on saving Killer that I never really paid much attention to the place. But now my earlier conversation with Bella has me curious.

The office is richly decorated, in an old-fashioned, leather and wood paneling kind of way. The walls are covered with certificates and awards and tons of photos of various humans. But, just as Bella said, none of them seem to have Antonio anywhere in the picture. And now that I'm seeing it all in person, I have to agree with Bella. It does all seem a bit odd.

After a few minutes of ignoring me, he evidently finishes his conversation and hangs up the phone. "So. Moose. Good you'se could make it down here to see me. I trust your trip was copacetic?"

Okay, the real Antonio is missing in action, once again. He's back to the whole Owen Wilson Godfather routine. "Yeah, no problems at all," I tell him. "Now that I know how to work the L train bit, I can move around the city pretty much at will. Even with the busted ear." I point to the white bandage covering the tip of my right ear.

"Yer ear? Yeah, I noticed that. What happened to ya? Get into a little tussle with a honey bee?"

I pick out a chair in front of Antonio's desk and hop on up. "Very funny, Antonio, very funny." I try to give him the most serious look I can manage, which I'll admit isn't all that much. "Actually, Bella and I had a little visit yesterday from a mutual friend of ours. And he certainly had some biting comments to share with us."

"Is dat so?" Antonio asks, slipping back and forth between his usual carefree jovial self and actually looking a little concerned for a change. "And who might dat be?"

“The last surviving member of the CC’s dynamic duo. Ralfie.”

The blood seems to drain from Antonio’s face. “Ralfie? The Doberman? How the heck did he find you?”

“I don’t know, Antonio. Only thing I can figure is that word must have gotten out onto the street about the prison break. About who might have been behind all that. Another dynamic duo altogether, a dog and a cat. Any idea how that might have hit the streets so fast?”

Antonio can’t help but glance over at his phone, and I know that I’m right. It was him.

“Look, Moose, I — I didn’t mean to cause no problems. Things have been a little tight around here lately, and I kinda need the business...”

“And let me guess, you spread your name around a little here and there about what we pulled off last week, and suddenly your phone’s ringing off the hook,” I venture.

“Well… I wouldn’t exactly say that.”

I'm not letting him off the hook, phone or not. "Did you or did you not spread the word that you and I were the brains behind the escape?"

He's staring at his paws, avoiding any possibility of looking in my direction. "Yeah, I might a said dis or dat."

"And Ralfie gets wind of all that, then suddenly shows up in Bella's backyard in the flesh, and as a result we came within a snail's line of snot of becoming somebody's can of Alpo," I finish for him.

Antonio is still having problems making eye contact with me right about now. And I can't blame him. About the eye contact, not about the reason he can't look at me. That point I'm laying right at his fat little feline feet.

"Look, Fat Tony, whatever happens to me, I can handle it. Heck, I've already done two long tours in Sing Sing, so I'm far from guiltless in this world. But Bella, she's another story. Your big mouth came within seconds of costing my sweet little Corgi her life. So what do you have to say about that?"

He takes a long time to respond, and when he does it comes out more like a mouse's tiny squeak than a cat's meow. "I got nothin' to say to that, Moose. Yer right. I screwed up. Big time. Got no excuses." He clears his throat and coughs up a small hairball into his ash tray. That seems to have settled him down a bit, and he's no longer fidgeting with his paws. "But look, Moose, all that aside, now we got an even bigger problem to deal with. The CC's, are they still after us? Do we need to talk with PETSEC about saving our own lives? Maybe pull Bella along with us?"

Being around Antonio suddenly has me completely exhausted. Especially that fake Italian accent, which has now almost completely evaporated again. "You know what, Antonio? Why don't you just come clean for a change? Why does everything always have to be some kinda game with you?"

He looks at me, confused. "Wuddaya mean? I'm being brutally honest wit ya, Moose. Always have been."

I give him a bitter smile. If it hadn't been for everything we've been through together this last week or so, I don't think I'd bother giving him even that.

"Look around you, Antonio. Bella was right. Not a single picture of you on the walls. Not one. And who the heck is this guy Michael Cheerio? Huh? Who's he?"

Antonio glances over at the wall to his left, and seems confused. "Cheerio?" Then his face clears. "Oh, you mean Shapiro. Yeah. Him." He bites down on his lower lip, thinking. After a long pause he nods his head oh so slightly and seems to have finally come to some kind of decision.

"Okay, Moose. No more lies. After everything you did last week, you deserve the truth. The whole truth." He points off to the left with one outstretched paw. "Shapiro? He's my human. My master. This right here is his law office. I scammed an extra key to the place off him a while back, so sometimes I sneak in here to use the joint when he's not around."

"So you're not really Gattogrosso after all?" I ask, completely dumbfounded now. "And Shapiro? I dated a girl with that name once. As I recall, she was Jewish—"

Antonio stands up and moves to the left around his desk, closing the distance between us. "Yeah. You're right. I'm not really Italian after all. Far from it. It was all just a big ruse. My real name's Anthony Shapiro."

"But — why?"

"For the oldest reason in the book, Moose. Money. When I first got started in this business, I hung out a shingle as Anthony Shapiro. Got a few cases here and there, but nothing to write home about. Not even enough to pay the bills. So I hired this high dollar marketing firm from down the street to give my business a complete makeover. They're the ones who came up with the whole idea of Fat Tony. They even cooked up the story about the Greyhound Mafia up in Evanston."

"The Greyhounds?" I'm stunned, almost speechless. Now I'm suddenly unsure of almost everything else I know about this world. "You mean none of that was real?"

"Oh, the Greyhounds were real, all right. Just not anything I had to do with. As a matter of fact, I've never been to Evanston in my entire life. So the puff writers, they just took a real story and inserted my new fake name right smack in the middle of it. Charged me a fortune, but it was well worth it. Now the whole city of Chicago knows my name. And as it turns out, they were right. A solid reputation, a good brand is all you really need to make a fortune in this business. Whether that reputation is based on reality or not."

Now it's my time to take a turn staring off into space, lost. "So, Tony. Anthony, whatever. Other than the fake story about Evanston, have you ever done anything big at all? Any real success stories?"

I feel a paw being laid softly on my right shoulder. "Just one, Moose. Just one."

"The Great Escape?" I suggest. "The case we worked together?"

"That's about it." He moves up next to me, both of us staring out the window, not yet willing to look each other in the eye. "So now you know the whole truth, Moose. Working with you is the only time I've ever really done anything that matters. Anything that made a bit of difference in the world."

"And yet you had to lie to me the whole time about everything. You didn't trust me with the truth."

"I was afraid, Moose. Afraid that if you knew the truth, if you knew what a big fat giant fraud I truly am, then there's no way you'd ever want to work with me. But I'll have to give it to you. You're one heck of a private eye. You took one hard look at this office and saw through my charade in a heartbeat. I had pulled the wool over the entire city of Chicago, but in the end I couldn't fool you."

All I'm thinking about right now is Bella. She's the one who really saw through all this. Just like she always seems to see right through me.

His hand drops off my shoulder as he moves away, circling back around the desk. "So I guess this means goodbye, Moose. And — about the tuna you owe me. Seeing as how everything you promised to pay me was all built upon false pretenses, built upon all my lies, I don't see how I really have any right to get paid for what little I did. So I guess we're even. I just wish this had all worked out a different way, is all. I've really enjoyed meeting you, working with you. Enjoyed our friendship, short as it was. And I only hope that someday you can find a way to forgive me."

I move around the desk as well to stand before him one last time at the window. I can feel his paw settle on my shoulder again as I stare down at the world of tiny little ants swarming around on the streets below us. I can see a single mother, juggling a tall stack of packages while still managing to steer her two little boys toward their car. A young couple is arguing outside of a sandwich shop. Everyday people, going about their everyday lives. Just like I was, before Penny got killed and everything went all crazy in my world. Before Bella became something more than just a silly flirtation.

I turn to face him one last time. "You know, Anthony, if there's one thing I've learned from all of this, if there's anything Bella has taught me over the years, it's that you're always better off being true to yourself, being true to what and who you really are, deep inside. Instead of trying to act like something you're not. Better off being the little guy everyone can count on, than always trying to come off as some kinda big shot. Mister Impotent. As that William Spearmint guy once said, all the world's a stooge. But that doesn't mean you have to be one, too."

I can feel a heavy weight falling off my shoulders as I turn around to leave. But it might have been just his paw. As I reach the hall outside, my steps have already begun to lighten a little. After all, I've accomplished everything I set out to do when I came here this morning, and more. In the process, I've lost what could have been a great friend. And it feels that I may have also lost a large part of the careless youth that I've been carrying around for so long inside of me, my playful little puppy sense of unbridled wonder. And that's probably a good thing.

I don't know if our business with the Crimson Canines is finally over, or if someday I'll have to face that nightmare once again. But what I do know is that I still have at least one friend, one true friend, who desperately needs my help. Maybe for the last time. And even better, I have a girl at home who somehow fills my life with a greater sense of wonder than any puppy's ever known. A girl who always finds a way to bring out the big puppy dog eyes in me, every time I see her. I may not be some kinda big shot in this world, but she sure makes me feel like the luckiest dog alive. Makes me feel like I'm a big shot in her world. And at the end of the day, that's the only world that will ever again matter to me.

Lysle, Illinois, Three Weeks Later

Fisheye and I are waiting in the bushes with Killer, watching. So far the little green and yellow house in front of us has been pretty quiet. The mailman came by earlier on and dropped off a few letters, which understandably created a few tense moments for Killer and I. But somehow Fisheye managed to keep a lid on both of us and we got through it with no unfortunate incidents.

It's been a long few weeks or so for all of us, although to be fair, PETSEC has done all the heavy lifting, even bouncing back and forth between Killer's safe house, Fisheye's office behind the grocery store and my own back yard to keep us all in the loop as to the progress they've been making. Not just with Killer, but with everyone else we liberated that night, now over three weeks in the past. It seems even longer. Like an eternity, sometimes, when I think back.

Fisheye and Ike have landed a low interest loan from PETSEC and are starting up some kind of nonprofit food delivery business, repackaging leftovers they find in the trash behind the city's restaurants and grocery stores and selling them to less resourceful cats and dogs. The kind of pets humans like to call strays, but in reality are just the mostly forgotten homeless. Folks who for whatever reason just aren't as lucky as we are, and would probably starve to death if someone didn't jump in to help. Someone like my new best buddies, Fisheye and Ike. Ike told me confidentially that they give away almost all of the food, but since their costs are pretty much zero, it all seems to work out.

And meanwhile we've got one of my oldest and dearest friends to give a little boost to today. Killer's been cleaned up and, to his everlasting chagrin, the folks at PETSEC have even sprayed a hint of cologne on him, just enough to cover up any lingering dog odor that might be clinging to his fur.

The next few minutes are critical, and nothing can be left to chance. PETSEC agents are monitoring several of the side windows, keeping track of where all of the humans are located inside the building. The master has already left for work, and the mistress — a student at a local community college — is finally getting things cleaned up and put away before leaving the house and dropping her daughter off at school. And then heading off to class herself.

We get the signal, and I push Killer forward out of the bushes. "Go on, buddy. It's time."

He hesitates, then shrugs his shoulders and saunters softly up the steps to the front door. One paw goes up, just like he's been taught, pressing the doorbell. I can hear a soft chime ringing lightly from inside the house, and in less than a minute or so the front door flies open and a young girl appears. Maybe six or seven, it's always hard to tell exactly when it comes to humans. She's wearing some kind of school uniform, solids and plaids and a white shirt, and her honey blonde hair is hanging down in pigtails on either side of her face.

I can see her mouth go slack, her eyes filled with shock and fear as she sees Killer for the first time. But then he whimpers, just as he's been trained, and leans in to give her tiny hand a gentle lick. He sits back, his stub tail wagging a mile a minute and his eyes opening impossibly wide. He whimpers again, then lifts his right paw up in the air like he wants to shake.

The little girl is clearly torn between running for her life or reaching out to pet him. Unfortunately, humans have this thing about training their children to never pet dogs they don't know, which is really quite closed minded of them and very self destructive. I mean, what if they taught their kids to never be friendly toward another *kid* they'd never met? Think about how well that'd go over in daycare.

Eventually, though, the moon eyes do the trick. Carefully, cautiously she moves forward. At just the right moment, Killer eases himself to the ground, exactly like we've practiced. He's still got the moon eyes, but now he looks much smaller, more delicate. Less of a threat. The little girl reacts to all of this by stretching out one tentative little hand. She touches the top of his head, and he lets out a low purring noise, a cute little trick the PETSEC psychologists taught him, part of their extensive research into human behavior. If you think about it, purrs make up well over ninety percent of what Ike calls a cat's adorability quotient, whatever the heck that is. Without the purrs, a cat is nothing more than a self-centered, ego-centric parasite. At least that's one dog's humble opinion. Your mileage may vary.

Anyway, back to the present, the fawning and the purring seem to be working. The little girl starts to pet Killer's head in earnest, and after a while he responds by reaching up to lick her cheeks. Before you know it she's giggling and hugging him tightly around the neck.

"Who's at the door, Catherine?" her mother calls from somewhere deep inside the house.

"It's a *puppy*, Mommy! And he's got no collar! Can we keep him?"

Acknowledgments

Sometimes books aren't so much written as they write themselves, and this would be one of them. Trying to survive the absolute pandemonium I call home would have been impossible if I couldn't let off some steam every now and then by anthropomorphically channeling the voices of Moose, Tony and the rest of the unrelentingly persistent brood of cats and dogs that have owned me over the years. I only hope they've enjoyed my friendship a tenth as much as I've enjoyed theirs.

Once again, this book would be unfit for human, canine or even feline consumption but for the love and attention it received from my amazing editor, Kara Vaught. Her mastery of the English language is second to none, and this book is an excellent testament to that, Moose's creative mangling of that language notwithstanding.

The cover design actually drove much of the literary content of the story, particularly the remarkable image of the cat on the front cover that I sourced from Allvectors.com. Having known a few Maine Coon cats in my life, it just seems to capture some ethereal essence of their spirit. If you've never adopted a Maine Coon before, well — you might want to think twice before you do. Just kidding! Kinda sorta…

As always, my everlasting thanks to Elizabeth, my greatest cheerleader, my inspiration, my best friend forever, and the keeper of my heart. And to Judy, who like Moose has somehow managed to squeeze four times a person's normal allocation of gentle soul and irrepressible spirit into one rather petite package. As the dedication page says, she has always been the glue that over the years has served to bind a world of people tightly together in friendship and love, the kind of person you can only hope to meet but once in your lifetime. If you're even that lucky.

And, last but certainly not least, thanks to my real inspiration for this book, a fifteen pound bundle of absolute terror named Moose. He may be gone but he will never be forgotten. And Heaven will never be the same.

About the Author

Rene Fomby practices criminal defense and civil litigation across the state of Texas. An accomplished member of the State Bar's Probono College, Rene takes on the nail-biting cases that most other lawyers turn away. More importantly, Rene is a winemaker, sailor, private pilot, helicopter dad and loving husband, and is currently owned by two dogs and one very feisty Maine Coon cat.

Other Books by Rene Fomby

Resumed Innocent

The Game of War

Coming Soon

Reflecting the Dead

Revelations, Revolutions